He didn't need to huff, or puff
or blow the house down ...
The big bad wolf just walked in the door.

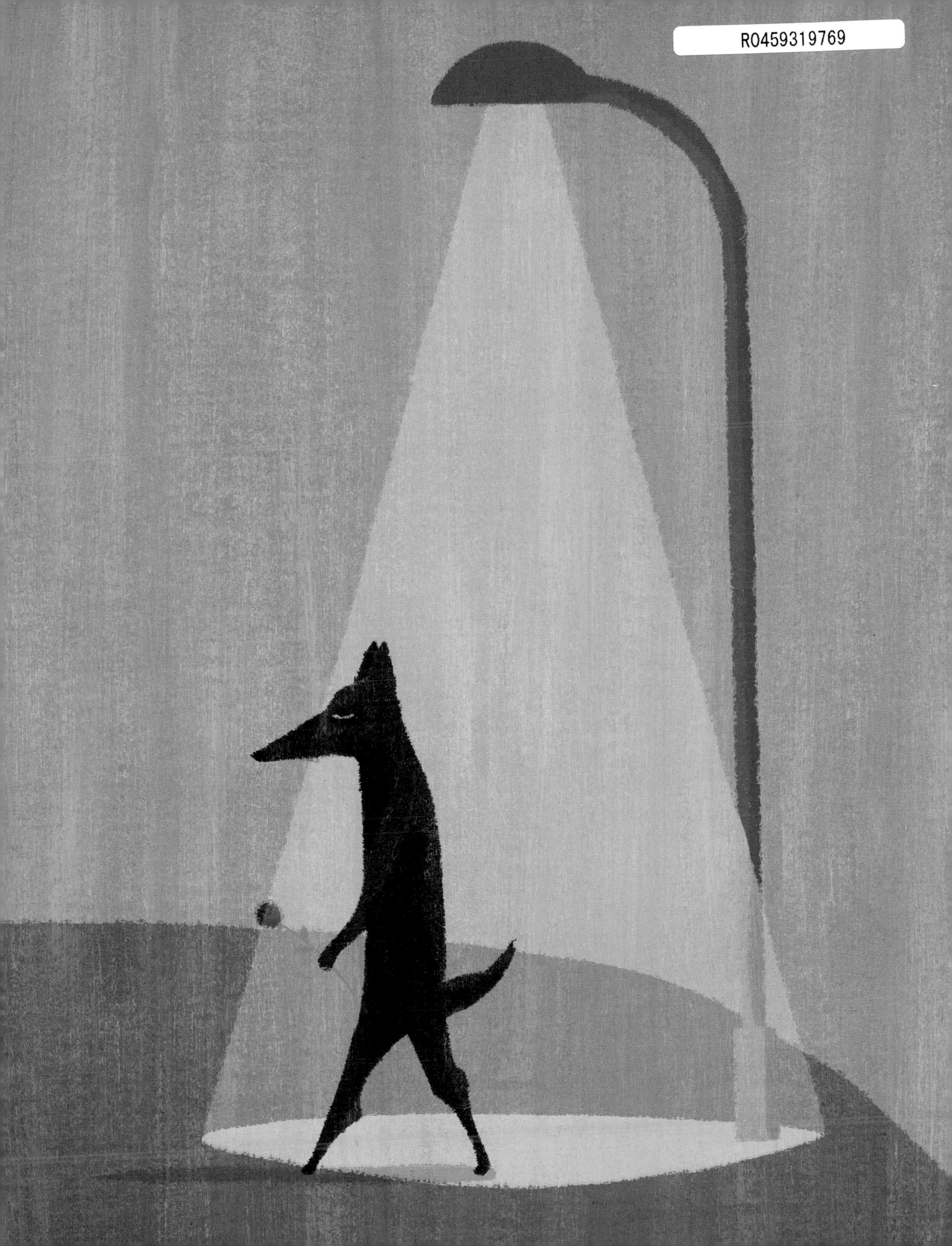

He batted his eyelashes and purred like a pussycat
in front of my mother.
But he looked at me with cold eyes and sharp teeth.
The honeymoon was sour, like lemons.

One day, my mother got home late.
She was out of breath as she told us how all the
traffic held her up.

The wolf was spitting mad, and he yelled bad names at her.
I won't repeat them, because I'm not allowed to say words like that.

That's when my mother's smile began to droop,

dragging her shoulders and her back down with it.

But that wolf did not tidy up anything.
He even threw his plate on the floor because
the pasta was cold.
At school, we clean up our messes and say sorry,
even if it's an accident.
This was no accident.

The wolf howled, too.
Not at the moon ...
He howled at my mother.

When he left finger marks on my arm, I had to cover them up with long sleeves, even when it was hot out.

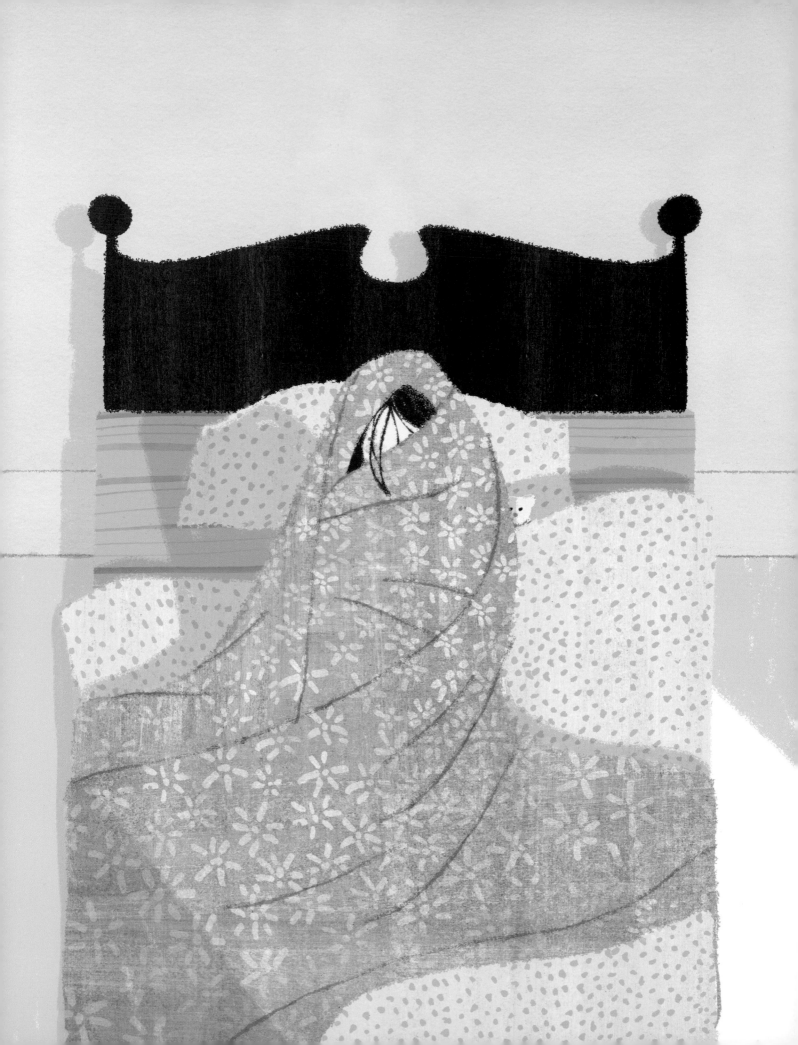

I built myself another house inside my little
bedroom, next to the living room.
But whenever the sounds of yelling and
breaking started, the blankets jumbled up
around my head did not protect me any
more than a pile of straw.

My bedroom door should have stopped him,
but he came in without knocking.
He paid no attention to a barrier made of wood.

So I built a fort made of bricks.
I put it up around my heart.
I closed my eyes and kept them closed,
even on the days when the sun came out again.

My eyes opened the day my mother handed me a suitcase
filled with my things.
"We're leaving," she said. "You have five minutes
to find Gilbert."

At the other house, a nice woman welcomed us in.
She put her arms around my mother. She showed
us our room. The kitchen was full of people
chatting.
Mothers, children.
But no wolves.

That night, I finally had a good sleep, even though my mother
was crying in her bed.
The big bad wolf can huff and puff all he wants,
but this house will not fall down.

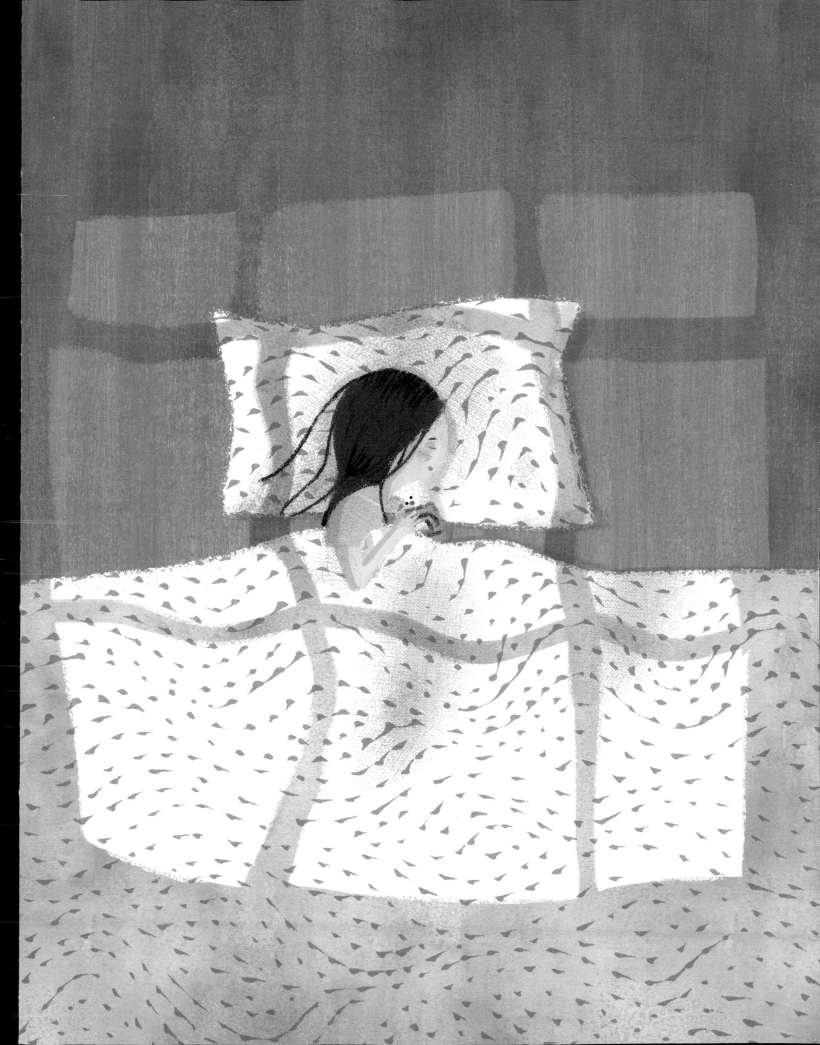

910ASA

AS/A2 GEOGRAPHY

CONTEMPORARY CASE STUDIES

This book is due for return on or before the date shown below.

KT-416-317

Rura... ...ent & t... ...de

Sue War...

Acknowledgement

I would like to thank Dulcie Knifton for her help and advice in producing this book, in particular, the section on leapfrogging.

Philip Allan Updates, an imprint of Hodder Education, an Hachette UK company, Market Place, Deddington, Oxfordshire OX15 0SE

Orders

Bookpoint Ltd, 130 Milton Park, Abingdon, Oxfordshire OX14 4SB
tel: 01235 827720
fax: 01235 400454
e-mail: uk.orders@bookpoint.co.uk

Lines are open 9.00 a.m.–5.00 p.m., Monday to Saturday, with a 24-hour message answering service. You can also order through the Philip Allan Updates website: www.philipallan.co.uk

© Philip Allan Updates 2010

ISBN 978-1-84489-208-2

First printed 2010
Impression number 5 4 3 2 1
Year 2015 2014 2013 2012 2011 2010

Front cover photograph © Tony Watson/Photographers Direct

Printed in Italy

Hachette UK's policy is to use papers that are natural, renewable and recyclable products and made from wood grown in sustainable forests. The logging and manufacturing processes are expected to conform to the environmental regulations of the country of origin.

Contents

Introduction

Part 1: The character of rural areas

Part 2: Changing environments

Part 3: Conflicts in the countryside

Part 4: Rural futures

Part 5: Examination advice

Index

Introduction

Although until very recently the majority of the world's people lived in rural areas, the emergence of rural geography as a specific branch of geography has only really happened since the 1980s, with the work of, for example, Cloke and Yarwood. It had been far more fashionable to study the urban world.

This book aims to redress the balance by looking at the radical changes taking place in rural areas, often breathtaking in their totality and pace. Rural areas across the world have very different geographies as a result of the diversity of their physical and human environments. The case studies have been chosen to show this variety. They emphasise that rural areas are complex and frequently contested environments, particularly at the **rural–urban fringe**, where rural meets urban.

The book also emphasises that many of the parallel changes being experienced in rural areas are a result of global processes — globalisation and rising levels of economic development (modernisation) — which have a huge impact on these areas as providers of food and resources and recreational opportunities, as well as facilitating a rural revolution in ICT. At the same time it emphasises that currently there are very significant differences between developed and developing areas.

People around the world have very different perceptions of rural areas — from places of beauty and tranquillity to areas beset by problems of **social exclusion**, hardship and poverty. The future of rural areas is a major concern for geographers and decision makers, and is therefore a main thrust of the book: as in the rest of the world, developing a sustainable future is a priority. Increasingly this may need to be achieved by radical rethinking. In many developed areas this involves a complete refocus, known as **rebranding**, whereby rural areas become landscapes which are primarily an object of consumption for recreation and business, predominantly by urban dwellers.

About this book

This book explores the dimensions of rural geography under four main headings: character, change, conflicts, and challenges for a sustainable future.

In Part 1, definitions of rurality are explored to emphasise the diversity of rural environments. The definition of 'rurality' (ruralness) varies within the **rural–urban continuum** from extremely remote, even wilderness areas through to very accessible, highly suburbanised peri-urban zones on the fringes of urban areas. The contrasting features of rural areas in developed and developing countries add to the variety of rural environments. The very diverse character of rural areas is a response to both physical and human influences, and the three case studies in this part have been selected to show both the variety of landscapes and the diversity of communities living in them.

In Part 2 the scale and pace of rural change are examined. Rural areas are subject to changes in their societies and economies, closely linked to changes occurring in urban areas. Figure 1 shows the ways in which rural and urban areas are interlinked. The rural areas supply the urban areas with food and resources, and at the same time are providers of leisure and recreation for urban people.

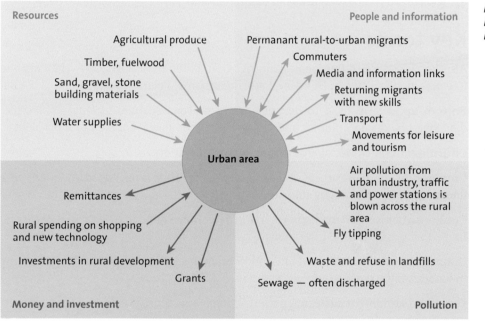

Figure 1
Rural–urban interlinkages

These changes are also closely linked to changes at a world scale of modernisation leading to increased urbanisation and industrialisation and to the forces of globalisation. While parallels can be observed between developing and developed nations, many of the outcomes are very different. NICs such as South Korea, Brazil, Mexico and China may make the differences even more blurred.

Rural conflicts are often associated with change. The traditional inhabitants and users of the countryside wish to preserve their way of life, and their values frequently conflict with those of newcomers who wish to use the countryside for different purposes and often support change. In the UK, for example, while the right to hunt with hounds is in many ways peripheral to the main conflicts between environmental conservation and countryside development, the 'Liberty and Livelihood' campaign of 2002 did cover the wider issues of concern over the scale, pace and direction of change.

In Part 3 the case studies explore a range of conflicts, such as those concerning the exploitation of resources and the contested environments of remote areas of outstanding beauty and the rural–urban fringe.

Part 4 considers the challenges facing rural areas. The challenges to a sustainable future for rural areas are very great, because of issues such as service provision in often sparsely populated areas and the alleviation of poverty in stricken areas. Overarching case studies therefore explore some of the key issues associated with innovative solutions for the future, which in some developed areas can lead to widespread rebranding. This part asks what exactly is a sustainable future for the countryside, as there are tensional forces between environmental, economic and socio-cultural sustainability.

Part 5 provides guidance on a number of problems that students come across when using case studies of rural areas in examinations.

Key terms

A8: the eight eastern European countries that joined the EU in 2004. They are the Czech Republic, Estonia, Hungary, Latvia, Lithuania, Poland, Slovakia and Slovenia.

Bottom-up: a term used to describe a scheme or initiative, usually small-scale, developed by the community and designed to offer a local solution to a problem.

Churning: frequent backwards and forwards migration.

Commodification: the process by which the countryside is packaged and marketed, usually for consumption by tourists.

Counterurbanisation: the increase in the percentage of people living in rural areas, fuelled by urban-to-rural migration.

Countryside stewardship: an environmentally friendly scheme that pays farmers to look after the countryside.

Dispersed settlement pattern: a pattern (usually low-density) of isolated settlements.

Edge cities: new suburban settlements built in the rural–urban fringe around existing cities.

Ecotourism: a type of tourism with key sustainable features.

Eco-towns: towns designed for sustainable living, with features such as zero carbon emissions.

Farm diversification: the process by which farmers develop alternative ways of making money to supplement their income from farming.

Green belt: an area around cities in which development is severely restricted in order to combat urban sprawl.

Greenfield site: an area of land that is used for development, but unlike a brownfield area has not previously been built on.

Index of Rurality: an index developed by Professor Cloke to assess how rural an area is.

Nucleated settlement pattern: a settlement pattern dominated by clustered villages.

Post-productive countryside: countryside where agriculture is not the dominant means of making money.

Rebranding: developing and marketing a new brand for an area of countryside by re-imaging (creating a new focus) in order to kick-start its regeneration (revival).

Rural deprivation: a state in which countryside dwellers experience inequalities through lack of income, opportunities (e.g. for work and services) and adequate transport.

Rural depopulation: the process by which the countryside fails to maintain population levels, fuelled by an ageing population and out-migration.

Rural idyll: an ideal place to live — the perception of the countryside as a place of beauty and tranquillity.

Rural turnaround: the point at which the countryside begins to revitalise, fuelled by in-migration and regeneration.

Rural–urban continuum: the imperceptible change along a transect from remote rural areas to highly urbanised areas.

Rural–urban fringe: a rapidly changing area round the edge of a town or city, where both rural and urban influences are present.

Social exclusion: the process by which certain groups and individuals are excluded from achieving a reasonable quality of life.

Technological leapfrogging: the process by which remote rural areas with low levels of development can bypass the lack of infrastructure — for example, areas without telephone landlines which exploit new technologies such as mobile phones and broadband in order to develop.

Top-down: a term used to describe a scheme or initiative, usually large-scale and capital-intensive, developed and financed by governments and TNCs to help a country develop (e.g. a mega-dam).

Vital Villages programme: a UK government scheme offering rural regeneration grants that local communities can apply for to revitalise their villages (parish plans, transport grants etc.).

Websites and further reading

Developed rural areas

- www.cpre.org.uk — Campaign to Protect Rural England.
- www.nfuonline.com (National Farmers Union) and www.face-online.org.uk (an agricultural education site) give details on agricultural change.
- www.countryside-alliance.org.uk supports the interests of rural dwellers.
- www.ruralcommunities.gov.uk has a range of information on rural communities, especially issues such as deprivation and inequality.
- www.naturalengland.org.uk is a mine of information on rural development.
- www.alva.org.uk provides statistics on visitor attractions.

- **www.environment-agency.gov.uk** has information on rural environments.
- **www.ruralnetuk.org/** and **www.ruralcommunities.gov.uk/** have information for country dwellers.
- **http://europa.eu** (EU portal) and **www.defra.gov.uk** have details of rural grant schemes such as LEADER and Objective One.
- **www.statistics.gov.uk** provides statistics on **rural deprivation**.

Full details of hundreds of local and regional websites are combined in *Rufus: The Rural Focus Yearbook*, published by the Commission for Rural Communities. This also includes useful details of local authority sites (such as **www.cornwall.gov.uk**, the Cornwall Council site).

Developing rural areas

- **www.dea.org.uk** is a useful website as it provides details of the 45 development education centres in the UK, which house large quantities of materials concerning overall development.
- **www.fao.org** provides useful information on agricultural schemes, as does **www.ifad.org**.
- **www.guardian.co.uk/katine/** gives an outstanding profile of rural change in a village in Uganda.

Useful books

Barker, D. (2007) *Advanced TopicMaster: Rural Settlements*, Philip Allan Updates.

Hill, M. (2003) *Rural Settlement*, Hodder Education.

Regan, C. (ed.) (2002) *80:20 Development in an Unequal World*, published by 80:20 Educating and Acting for a Better World and Teachers in Development Education.

Woods, M. (2005) *Rural Geography*, Sage Publications.

Yarwood, R. (2002) *Countryside Conflicts*, Geographical Association.

The character of rural areas

Defining rurality

The definition of rurality depends to a great extent on which part of the world the person doing the defining comes from, and what their experience of rural living is. For example, the chocolate-box vision of black and white buildings and cosy pubs around a village green surrounded by beautiful fields and orchards is very 'English'. Alternatively, the idea of a rural area as a remote mountain wilderness, a place for camping and trekking, is very Californian. Yet again, a subsistence farmer in sub-Saharan Africa might associate rural areas with grinding poverty and a constant battle against food and water insecurity.

Essentially, definitions are either empirical, whereby land use and demographic characteristics are measured to classify the area for planning and development purposes, or conceptual, in which case they do not use quantitative measures but rely instead on social constraints, which have to do with how people imagine the countryside.

Figure 1.1 shows some conceptual definitions by English country dwellers in 2007, illustrating the case in which 'rural' is more a state of mind.

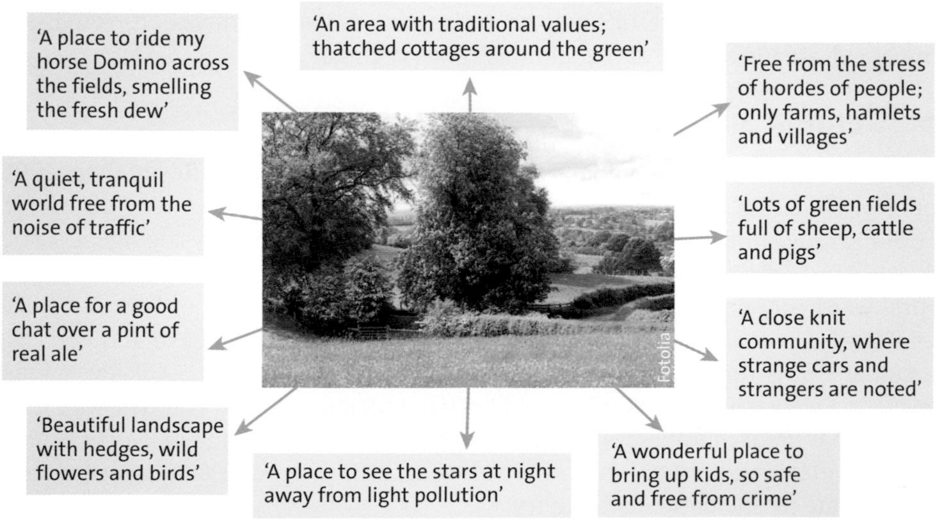

Figure 1.1
Conceptual definitions of English rurality

'A place to ride my horse Domino across the fields, smelling the fresh dew'

'An area with traditional values; thatched cottages around the green'

'Free from the stress of hordes of people; only farms, hamlets and villages'

'A quiet, tranquil world free from the noise of traffic'

'Lots of green fields full of sheep, cattle and pigs'

'A place for a good chat over a pint of real ale'

'A close knit community, where strange cars and strangers are noted'

'Beautiful landscape with hedges, wild flowers and birds'

'A place to see the stars at night away from light pollution'

'A wonderful place to bring up kids, so safe and free from crime'

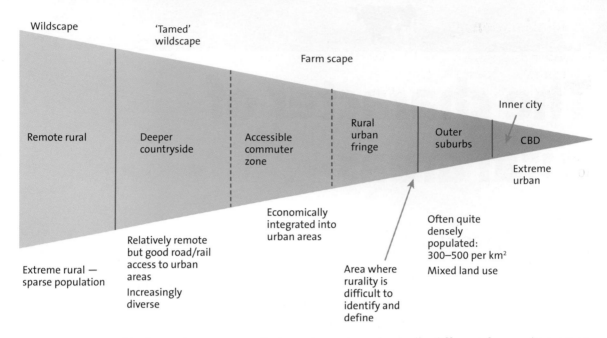

Wildscape

'Tamed' wildscape

Farm scape

Inner city

Remote rural

Deeper countryside

Accessible commuter zone

Rural urban fringe

Outer suburbs

CBD

Extreme urban

Extreme rural — sparse population

Relatively remote but good road/rail access to urban areas

Increasingly diverse

Economically integrated into urban areas

Area where rurality is difficult to identify and define

Often quite densely populated: 300–500 per km²

Mixed land use

Figure 1.2
The rural–urban continuum

Most people are aware that rural areas are basically different from urban areas, especially when they think in terms of the extreme ends of the rural–urban spectrum. The reality is that there is a continuum between the countryside and the town (Figure 1.2), and that quantitative techniques are needed to justify the exact reasons for designating an area as either rural or urban.

When defining an area as rural, we can use a number of criteria, such as settlement size and administrative function, population density or sparsity, access to services, land use and degree of built-up land/availability of open spaces, nature of employment and peripherality (degree of isolation).

Alternatively, as no one single criterion is necessarily reliable, multi-variate analysis can be used to define degrees of rurality on the basis of a combination of indicators. Inevitably, the availability of empirical measures is linked to a spatial unit such as a parish or a ward, so the results may be misleading, as the resulting choropleth maps imply a dramatic change at the administrative boundary.

Settlement size

Many countries employ a population threshold (for example, fewer than 2000 people) to define whether a settlement should be considered rural. In England, administrative units such as parishes (fewer than 1000 — Countryside Agency) and wards (fewer than 5000 — rural health research) are used, but problems arise if a rural ward contains one or more villages, or is in a mining area or is on the edge of a large urban area. Other countries use different limits: in Greece and Portugal a settlement is rural if it has fewer than 10000 people; in the USA if fewer than 2500; in Sweden if fewer than 500 and in Denmark if fewer than 200. This variation shows that small numbers are not enough to define a settlement as rural, and that the maximum critical threshold varies according to what is administratively appropriate for the particular country.

Population density

Population density is a very widely used criterion, as it is easy to calculate the figure and to make comparisons. However, density gives an average for an area and may be misleading, as it ignores population distribution within a spatial unit. In the UK, Standard Spending Assessments (SSAs), which apportion grants to local authorities, measure sparsity and super-sparsity. In contrast to urban areas, rural areas are not built up, and therefore densities are characteristically under 300 per km² (250 per km² in Norway), in contrast to heavily urbanised areas that reach densities of over 10 000 per km². However, some rural areas in developing nations such as Java have over 1000 people per km².

Land use

Rural areas have a low percentage of built-up land, and usually consist of up to 60% open spaces, such as green fields. This openness of aspect is one of the easiest ways people can identify rural areas.

The Council of Europe defines a rural area as 'a stretch of inland or coastal countryside, including small farms and villages, where the main part of the area is used for primary activity or economic and social activities such as country crafts, or non-urban recreation and tourism'. This definition thus employs land use as a key criterion.

Function (access to services)

In general, rural areas have a narrower range of functions, and these functions are usually low-order in comparison with those of towns (basics such as primary school, post office, pub etc.). Within rural areas, market towns and large villages assume the role of key settlements, where planners guarantee access to a broad basket of important services for all rural dwellers in the surrounding catchment area. Techniques such as the index of centrality can be used to quantify service levels.

Peripherality

The concept of peripherality is often seen as a means of distinguishing between extreme (remote) rural areas and those that are more accessible. Criteria of terrain, climate and physical barriers such as coastlines, mountains, poor roads and remoteness are all important in defining this quality. Tranquillity (Figure 1.3) is one of the key criteria of more remote areas and is quite closely linked to the degree to which an area is built up.

Employment

Employment is often seen as fundamental in establishing how rural an area is. Traditionally, the main source of employment in rural areas has been primary (farming, fishing and forestry). When designating an area as urban, some countries (e.g. Israel) place an upper limit on the percentage employed in agriculture (usually 15–20%). In developed countries there are growing numbers of people working

Figure 1.3
*Index of tranquillity
for England*

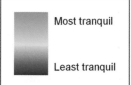

Most tranquil

Least tranquil

Kilometres
0   25 50   100   150   200

in services and manufacturing in rural areas; in some rural areas under 2% work directly in agriculture but a higher percentage are employed in agriculture-related activities.

It has become clear that the empirical measures suggested apply largely to rural areas in developed countries, and that no one criterion can encapsulate the essentials of rurality in all types of area.

Pioneering work was done in the 1970s by Cloke, whose **Index of Rurality** identified a series of indicators of rural life appropriate for that period. These were derived

Table 1.1 *Cloke's Index of Rurality*

1971 indicator	Rural area	Commentary today
Occupational structure — percentage of farmers and farm workers	High	Still likely to be higher in most rural areas, but declining
Population over 65 years old	High	Still useful — rural areas do have a high percentage of pensioners
Population density	Low	Still lower than urban areas, but some rural areas are very urbanised, with medium population density
Household amenities, i.e. percentage with hot water, fixed bath	High	Not very useful now, as all houses tend to have these
Percentage of total population aged 15–45 years	Low	Still useful; but 20–45 years is more accurate, because most people stay in education until 18 years old
Occupancy rate: percentage of population at 1.5 people per room	Low	Still applicable because of smaller households and larger houses (cheaper land)
Percentage of population resident for less than 5 years	Low	Not applicable now, since so many people are moving to villages (counterurbanisation)
Percentage of people working outside the settlement	Low	Not true for commuter villages: many people have to travel out for work
Distance from nearest urban centre of 50 000 people	High	Still likely to be applicable
Percentage change in population 1951–61, 1961–71	Decrease	Not since 1971, as rural populations overall are increasing in many areas

from census and cartographic data. Initially 16 indicators were used, but these were refined to ten key indicators. Some 40 years later the rate of rural change means these indicators are of less use. Table 1.1 summarises the indicators and suggests their current usefulness

The following new indicators to define remote rural areas have been suggested to update the index for 2010. What do you think?

- poor reception of at least one mobile phone company's signal
- poor access to high-speed broadband
- at least 45 minutes' journey to an Accident and Emergency department at a hospital
- over 15 km to major services such as high school, bank or major supermarket
- no regular bus service on a daily basis
- designation as one of CPRE's tranquil areas
- low percentage of commuters to urban areas

1

Using case studies

(a) Evaluate the suggested replacements for a new and up-to-date version of Cloke's index.
(b) Select five indicators from Cloke's original 1970s index to include in a new index for today. Justify your choice.
(c) Draw a conceptual diagram of how rural dwellers in a developing country might see their environment. Use Figure 1.1 as a starting point.
(d) Develop an index for the assessment of rurality in developing countries. Justify your choice. Use the UNDP database (or similar) to gain an insight into likely indicators for health, education, poverty levels etc.

In 1994, a rurality index derived by Dr Charles Cleland, was the first attempt in the USA to assess how rural each of the 48 mainland states was.

Ten factors were finally selected from over 150 possibles to determine each state's rurality, namely:

■ level of difficulty in reaching a large retail outlet such as Wal-Mart
■ degree of access to metropolitan (urban) areas by interstate highway
■ education level of citizens (lower in rural areas)
■ percentage of citizens employed in retail trade, professional or related services or public services
■ median family income
■ incidence of poverty (often high in rural areas)
■ number of local newspapers
■ recent population growth (very slow in rural areas)
■ popularity of the local country as a retirement destination
■ population density

The index was needed to enable social services and government agencies to identify the more isolated and extreme rural areas, as previously the only available definition was a crude one: a 'county' with fewer than 2500 people was defined as a rural area.

Questions

(a) Assess the suitability of the ten chosen criteria. Would they be suitable for use in areas other than the USA?

(b) Use Figure 1.4 to describe, and suggest reasons for, the distribution of rurality in Oregon.

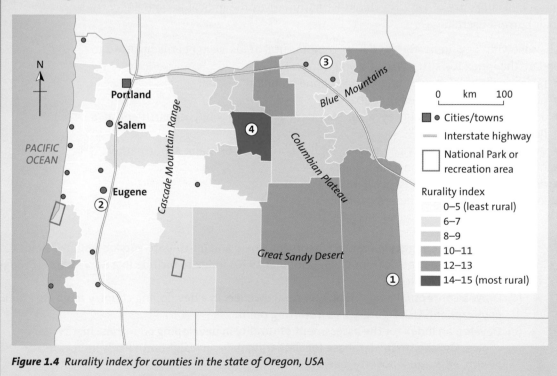

Figure 1.4 *Rurality index for counties in the state of Oregon, USA*

In 2000 Cloke defined 'rural' as: 'areas which are dominated by extensive land uses such as agriculture and forestry, or by large open spaces or underdeveloped land which contain small, lower-order settlements demonstrating a strong relationship between buildings and extensive landscape, and *which are perceived as rural by most residents* — thus combining the empirical and the conceptual'.

Contrasting rural geography in developed and developing nations

While we do not wish to stereotype the differences between developed and developing countries, there is no doubt that there are very significant contrasts, and the issues facing their rural areas can be very different.

Figures 1.5 (a) and (b) show the contrasting **rural–urban continuums**. The contrasts result from:

- differences in flows of population
- differing levels of income
- different styles of economy

Table 1.2 summarises some of the essential contrasts shown.

Note that while Table 1.2 emphasises contrasts, it also shows that some of the sustainable solutions can be very comparable across all states of development. The section in Part 4 on the role of technology in developing rural areas emphasises some of the parallel issues regarding the need to develop sustainable solutions.

Developing rural–urban balance

In 2005 for the first time there were more people living in urban areas of the world than in rural areas, as a result of rapid urbanisation in the developing world. Nevertheless, in both absolute and relative terms, the vast majority of rural dwellers live in the 'Global South' as defined by the Brandt Line.

There are just over 300 million rural inhabitants, representing over 26% of the total population, living in the Global North, in contrast to 3 billion rural inhabitants in the Global South. The changes over time are summarised by Figure 1.6.

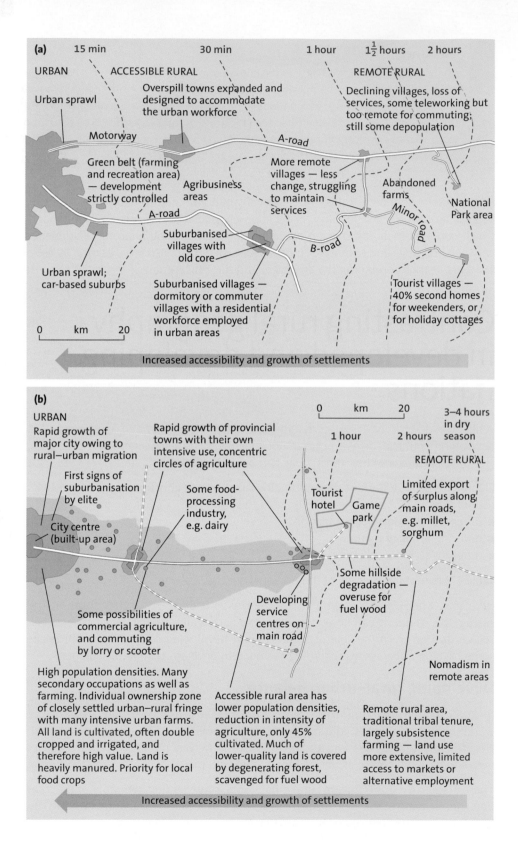

(a)

15 min   30 min   1 hour   1½ hours   2 hours

URBAN   ACCESSIBLE RURAL   REMOTE RURAL

Urban sprawl

Overspill towns expanded and designed to accommodate the urban workforce

Declining villages, loss of services, some teleworking but too remote for commuting; still some depopulation

Motorway   A-road

Green belt (farming and recreation area) — development strictly controlled

Agribusiness areas

More remote villages — less change, struggling to maintain services

Abandoned farms

National Park area

A-road

Minor road

Suburbanised villages with old core

B-road

Urban sprawl; car-based suburbs

Suburbanised villages — dormitory or commuter villages with a residential workforce employed in urban areas

Tourist villages — 40% second homes for weekenders, or for holiday cottages

0   km   20

← Increased accessibility and growth of settlements

(b)

0   km   20

3–4 hours in dry season

URBAN

Rapid growth of major city owing to rural–urban migration

Rapid growth of provincial towns with their own intensive use, concentric circles of agriculture

1 hour   2 hours

REMOTE RURAL

First signs of suburbanisation by elite

Some food-processing industry, e.g. dairy

Tourist hotel

Game park

Limited export of surplus along main roads, e.g. millet, sorghum

City centre (built-up area)

Developing service centres on main road

Some hillside degradation — overuse for fuel wood

Some possibilities of commercial agriculture, and commuting by lorry or scooter

Nomadism in remote areas

High population densities. Many secondary occupations as well as farming. Individual ownership zone of closely settled urban–rural fringe with many intensive urban farms. All land is cultivated, often double cropped and irrigated, and therefore high value. Land is heavily manured. Priority for local food crops

Accessible rural area has lower population densities, reduction in intensity of agriculture, only 45% cultivated. Much of lower-quality land is covered by degenerating forest, scavenged for fuel wood

Remote rural area, traditional tribal tenure, largely subsistence farming — land use more extensive, limited access to markets or alternative employment

← Increased accessibility and growth of settlements

Table 1.2 *Summary of contrasts*

Characteristic	Developing areas	Developed areas
Population	Between 30 and 80% live in rural areas. While birth rates remain high (average 2.6% per annum natural increase), since 2000 the rate has been decreasing. This, combined with high rural-to-urban migration rates and the incidence of famine and HIV/AIDS, means that rural populations are in relative decline in many areas, and in some areas (e.g. Darfur in Sudan) there is an absolute decline.	Between 10% and 30% of people live in rural areas. Many rural areas, especially accessible areas, are increasing in population because of urban-to-rural migration (counterurbanisation). Rates of increase vary, as in many cases in-migration is largely of the 50-plus age group whereas 18–35-year-olds are still moving to cities. In remoter, less favourable areas rural depopulation is continuing to occur.
Employment	Many rural dwellers (c. 40–80%) are subsistence farmers or fishermen. Manufacturing remains limited although options for service employment (e.g. in tourism) are increasing.	Variety of employment, with under 10% employed as farmers or in farm-related work. Range of rural manufacturing and businesses, rising opportunities in tourism. Increasing numbers of telecommuters are working from remote areas.
Services	Generally poor level of services, such as clinics and schools. Many people drawn to urban areas for these reasons. Often poor infrastructure.	Some problems in providing efficient private and public services (often declining), largely because of high cost and almost universal car ownership that favours market towns.
Poverty and deprivation	High levels of poverty (under $1 a day) and deprivation in many areas. Ever-present issues of famine and environment-related disasters.	Pockets of absolute poverty (usually elderly people) known as 'hidden others'. Overall greater wealth on average than urban areas. Social exclusion exists because of mobility and opportunity deprivation.
Futures	Innovative solutions include the use of intermediate (appropriate) technology, which can increase incomes and improve daily life, e.g. micro-hydros. Need for sustainable solutions to provide alternative employment. Rather a bleak future, especially in times of world recession, as dependent on aid/investment.	Innovative solutions are required, especially finding new ways of service provision and maintaining quality of life for remote communities. Wide-ranging changes to a post-productive, pluri-activity landscape. Consumption of rural areas for leisure and tourism a key development. Many are optimistic about the future.

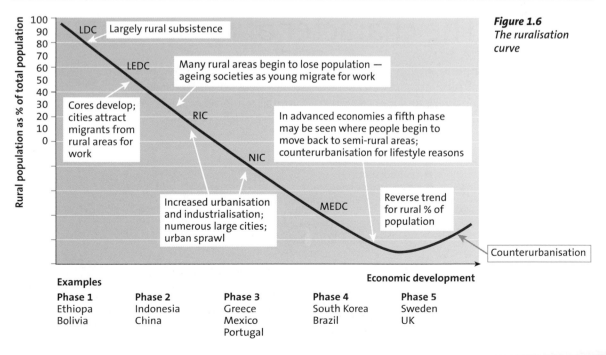

Figure 1.6
The ruralisation curve

Table 1.3 *Rural population by region and development grouping 1950–2030*

	1950		1975		2000		2005		Projected 2030	
	Population (million)	%	Population (million)	%	Population (million)	%	Population (million)	%	Population (million)	%
Africa	191	85.3	310	74.6	518	63.6	559	61.7	729	49.3
Asia	1162	83.2	1820	76	2313	62.9	2352	60.2	2236	45.9
Europe	271	49.5	232	34.4	206	28.3	203	27.8	152	21.7
Latin America	97	58	125	38.8	129	24.6	127	22.6	113	15.7
North America	62	36.1	64	26.2	66	20.9	64	19.3	53	13.3
Oceania	5	38	6	28.5	9	29.5	10	29.2	11	26.2
Global North	390	47.9	350	33.1	320	26.8	310	25.9	240	19.2
Global South	1400	81.9	2210	73.1	2920	59.7	3000	57.1	3050	43.9
World rural	**1790**	**71**	**2560**	**62.8**	**3240**	**53.3**	**3310**	**51.3**	**3290**	**40.1**
World total	**2520**		**4070**		**6090**		**6460**		**8200**	

As a result of continued high fertility in south Asia and Africa the absolute total of rural dwellers rose dramatically from 1.8 billion in 1950 to 3.3 billion in 2005, but in relative terms it declined from 71% to 51.3% — as shown in Table 1.3.

Note that Table 1.3 shows how the trends are expected to continue until 2030: it is projected that from 2005 there will be both an absolute decline and a sharp relative decline to 40% of the total population.

The character of rural areas

*Figure 1.7
Factors that
influence the rural
landscape*

In this section you can look at the contrasting pictures and accompanying maps of rural areas. They characteristically show rural landscapes and settlements, but look very different. Figure 1.7 summarises some of the factors that account for the differences.

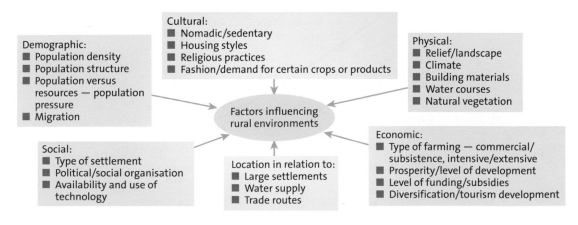

OUTBACK AUSTRALIA

Outback Australia is often referred to by Australians as 'beyond the back of Bourke' (which itself is a very small isolated town in northwest New South Wales). Common physical images of the outback include endless vistas of red desert with empty tracks and occasional road trains, while cultural images include the land of big thirsts with piles of beer cans, or small Aboriginal tribal settlements and economically huge sheep or cattle stations (some the size of Belgium), or mining settlements for iron ore or diamonds — big holes in a sea of desert surrounded by company-owned towns for the migrant workforce.

Characteristics of the remote, sparsely populated land include the following:

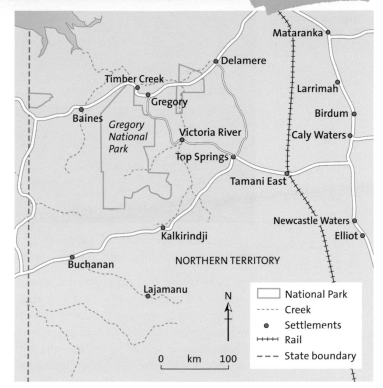

Figure 1.8
Outback Australia

■ The physical environment is difficult, which suppresses economic activity and repels residential settlement except for resource-based developments. The inhospitable lands support densities of as low as 2 per km², largely farming extensively low-yield agricultural land, often on a monocultural basis and usually for cattle.

■ Provision of services is difficult and costly, and frequently requires government assistance and innovative technology such as the Royal Flying Doctor Service, satellite technology and broadband for the provision of online services, and radio for the School of the Air. Nevertheless there is still the problem of distance to overcome, with a 500 km round trip to a supermarket. Mail orders and post are usually delivered weekly by plane or mail truck, with all stations having a flying strip. Major shopping expeditions usually happen only two or three times a year, necessitating a round trip of over 1000 km in a pick-up truck or van.

■ Social contact is vital so, amazingly, these scattered communities do get together, usually four or five times a year, for agricultural events such as gymkhanas or rodeos, which form part of the cultural fabric.

■ Many areas are declining in population, largely as a result of out-migration of the young people. This is in spite of a whole range of government schemes such as the Sustainable Regions Program or the Assistance for Isolated Child Scheme, which were designed to support the outback communities.

■ It is sometimes possible to see evidence of abandoned cattle stations from aerial surveys. Reasons for their abandonment include problems with hurricanes and other adverse weather (e.g. recurring drought with a very unpredictable water supply), falling farm prices, very limited employment prospects as services close, and

Figure 1.9
Long, straight
roads are used as
emergency landing
strips for the flying
doctor service

degradation of marginal lands. It is also possible to discern new homestay developments for tourists, as many stations have diversified to survive.

The 1994 Native Title Act enabled Aboriginal groups to reclaim land when the leases came up for renewal (2005–10 was a major period for this), and many tribal groups are beginning to manage the cattle stations where they once were stockmen. There are also grants dedicated to Aboriginal development, as some 27% of all aborigines live in rural areas in sprawling settlements with fewer than 500 people. As they contain nearly four times the number of people living below the poverty line compared with the average for Australia, they are in huge need of development projects such as the Centres for Aboriginal Culture and Education.

In summary, this is a rectangular landscape, with straight roads and fields similar to those of the American Prairies (a reflection of its history of settlement in the late nineteenth century), and very sparse population densities that reflect the harshness of the physical environment (Figures 1.8 and 1.9).

Case study 2 RURAL BRITTANY

In the 1950s Brittany was a somewhat backward and neglected part of France; a peripheral peninsula, poorly connected to the rest of the country, with an overwhelmingly rural focus on small-scale 'mixed' farming. The maritime climate gave rise to a green, largely pastoral landscape. The ancient *bocage* system, with small scattered fields surrounded by hedgerows, led to a very distinctive appearance (Figure 1.10). The settlement pattern was one of dispersed, quite densely scattered farms, each served by a village such as Plumeliau (Figure 1.11(a)). Out-migration, as a result of limited rural employment opportunities, had been occurring for over 100 years, so abandoned farms were a common feature.

Regional planning policy and EU grants have enabled Brittany to modify its economy, especially in the accessible southern coastal corridor where improvements in infrastructure, together with financial incentives to develop manufacturing, tourism and other service industries, allowed Brittany's economic base to broaden, leading to a much denser but still **dispersed settlement pattern**.

Elenathewise/Fotolia

Figure 1.10
Bocage landscape

Accessibility is the key to a two-speed Brittany, in which all the coastal zones, and other areas within commuting distance of the growth poles of Vannes, St Brieuc, Rennes and Brest, have experienced rapid change into more heavily built-up areas, with modernised agriculture, whereas the interior, more remote areas are almost unchanged and still exhibit the traditional *bocage* landscape.

Figure 1.11 (b) shows how the modernisation of agriculture has changed the landscape. The plots of individual farmers have undergone reparcelling (*remembrement*) with the help of EU grants to consolidate and also increase the size of farms to make them more efficient.

Figure 1.11
The Breton landscape around Plumeliau in (a) the 1950s and (b) the 1990s

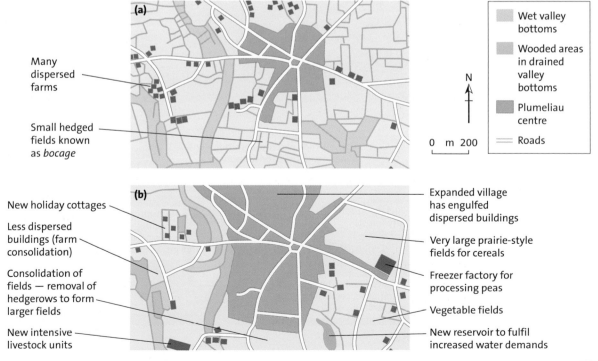

(a)

Many dispersed farms

Small hedged fields known as *bocage*

	Wet valley bottoms
	Wooded areas in drained valley bottoms
	Plumeliau centre
	Roads

N

0   m   200

(b)

New holiday cottages

Less dispersed buildings (farm consolidation)

Consolidation of fields — removal of hedgerows to form larger fields

New intensive livestock units

Expanded village has engulfed dispersed buildings

Very large prairie-style fields for cereals

Freezer factory for processing peas

Vegetable fields

New reservoir to fulfil increased water demands

The key to understanding settlement in the High Andes of Peru, Bolivia and Ecuador is the strong environmental gradients. The altitude of many of the communes or districts varies between 800 m and nearly 5000 m (Figures 1.12 (a) and (b)). The area has a highly **nucleated settlement pattern**, with a major service centre of around 1500 people located in a central position in the communes, and nearly all other people living in hamlets and villages. In the example shown, around 60% of the total population of 2500 live in San Pedro, the main settlement. The valley shown is very compact, so desert, mountain and cloud forest environments are all within a day's walk of San Pedro. The changes in temperature with altitude and rainfall amounts (note the arid west and the more humid east) have a major influence on the pattern of farming (Figure 1.12 (b)), leading to marked zonation of activities.

Figure 1.12
(a) The High Andes and (b) section across San Pedro District Commune showing the impact of 'environmental gradients'

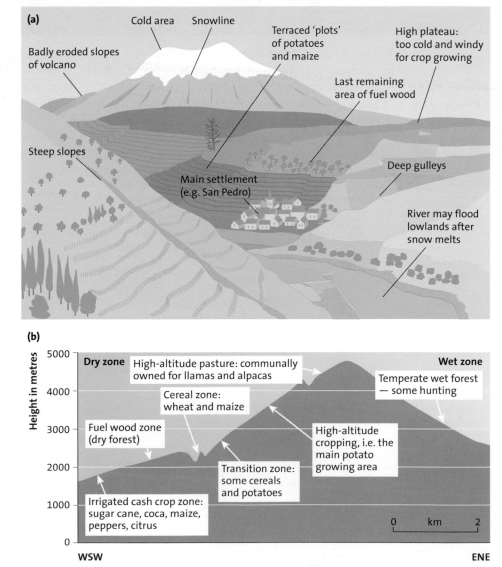

Anna Stowe Travel/Alamy

Figure 1.13
Landscape of the High Andes

   Farming could be described as sophisticated subsistence. The families have individual plots for growing cereals, vegetables and potatoes, but the high-altitude pasture is communally owned. The population is almost exclusively 'Indian', with adult literacy rates of around 20% even in Quechua, the native language. Agriculture is labour-intensive, and the community works together, exchanging labour on the basis of kinship and friendship, as the various tasks require (such as rice harvesting or potato picking). As the hillsides are so steep, terracing is a dominant feature for maize, wheat and vegetables. Individual holdings are very small (around 3 hectares).

   Many NGOs, such as Action Aid, are working in the High Andes to introduce a range of projects to improve the quality of life of the rural people. These include extending irrigated farming so that more cash crops can be grown, and developing micro hydro plants to provide power for rural enterprises such as knitting and weaving alpaca and llama wool. Microfinance schemes enable the local people to establish centres for using fertilisers and also to improve the quality of the seed potatoes they grow, of which there are many different kinds. Even today the valley is connected by a network of dirt tracks rather than tarmac roads, so transport is frequently by mule or on foot, especially to the high-level communal pastures, which in the future may be transformed into ranches.

(a) Look at Figure 1.7 again. Devise a table that summarises physical, demographic, social, economic and cultural factors that have contributed to the different characteristics of the three landscapes covered in the case studies.

(b) Write a comparison of the three areas under the headings of landscape, land use and settlement.

Guidance

(a) Try to include as many detailed facts as possible.

(b) Use all resources. Landscape can include relief, drainage and vegetation; land use should cover all types. For settlement use technical language to describe the patterns (nucleated/dispersed etc.) as well as description of settlement hierarchy.

Changing environments

Factors leading to change

In both developed and developing countries rural areas are undergoing rapid socio-cultural and economic changes. These changes have an impact on the communities, economy and environment. Driving many of these changes are demographic factors such as population dynamics and migration.

Agriculture (Figure 2.1) was traditionally the mainstay of rural life, but in many rural environments, almost always in developed areas, it has now been pushed more to the margins of the rural economy in terms of employment and its contribution to production. As we shall see in Part 4, in the future it is likely that many rural landscapes will become **post-productive**, with consumption and protection of rural environments more important than production. Inevitably the direction of change affects the quality of the rural environment.

The following case studies will therefore explore first changing population, second changing communities and services, and third the changing rural economy. Overall the changes are known as rural restructuring because of their intensity, their rapidity and the totality of their impact in many areas. They not only operate at a local scale, to produce more diverse rural environments, but also result from national and global factors, in particular, technological innovation and government policies as well as social modernisation and globalisation.

Figure 2.1
Players and factors influencing the changing agricultural economy

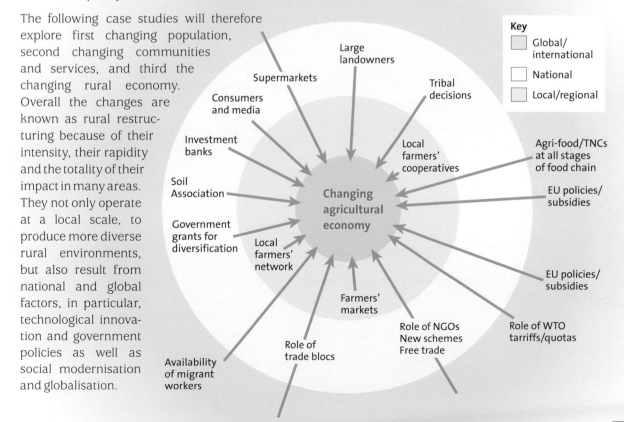

Key
- Global/international
- National
- Local/regional

Large landowners
Supermarkets
Tribal decisions
Consumers and media
Investment banks
Local farmers' cooperatives
Agri-food/TNCs at all stages of food chain
Soil Association
Changing agricultural economy
EU policies/subsidies
Government grants for diversification
Local farmers' network
Farmers' markets
EU policies/subsidies
Role of trade blocs
Role of NGOs New schemes Free trade
Role of WTO tarriffs/quotas
Availability of migrant workers

For example, if we are looking at agricultural change, as shown by Figure 2.1, the farmer is only one of a series of players operating at a range of scales, which influence or even control the direction of change.

Changing population: overview

In developed areas the overall trend has been, until recently, rural-to-urban migration, which, depending on the scale and pace, has traditionally led to **rural depopulation**. In general it is the productive, fertile element of the population that migrates to gain the greater opportunities and economic rewards offered by urban areas. However, a reversal of the flow was first noted in North America in the 1960s and soon spread to western Europe in the 1970s, then to other areas such as southeast Australia. This reverse flow, known as **counterurbanisation**, involves the movement of people from large towns initially to accessible rural areas, thus beginning the **rural turnaround**.

As most of the in-migrants were middle-class professionals with families, this stemmed rural depopulation and often led to a steady increase in population. While the flows were at their greatest in the 1970s and 1980s, they have continued until the present day, in spite of moves to encourage reurbanisation in the city centres for young professionals. By the 1990s counterurbanisation had spread to more remote areas with the advent of retirement migration to coastal districts and attractive market towns. This influx adds numbers to the population, but does little for growth. A further strand is provided by teleworkers, who can operate anywhere with a fast broadband connection. Many choose lifestyle migration (amenity migration) for their families and enjoy the **rural idyll**, and if sufficient volumes occur this can stem rural depopulation, especially if there is no significant outflow of the traditional young rural dwellers who are often forced out by a lack of employment and affordable housing.

So the balance between significant population growth in rural areas and significant rural depopulation is a fine one, varying from place to place and over time in one location.

Figure 2.2
Population change in rural areas in developed countries

Figure 2.2 shows the impacts of demographics and migration flows on population in developed countries.

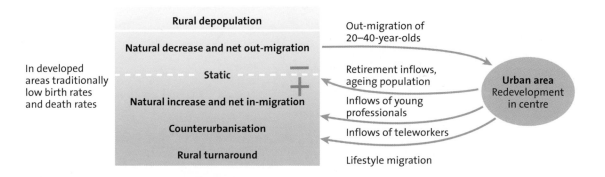

The case studies chosen illustrate the variations in population change, as shown.

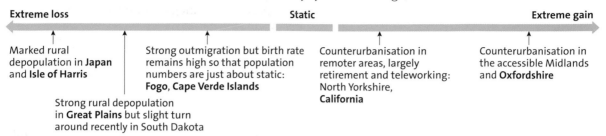

Extreme loss — **Static** — **Extreme gain**

Marked rural depopulation in **Japan** and **Isle of Harris**

Strong rural depopulation in **Great Plains** but slight turn around recently in South Dakota

Strong outmigration but birth rate remains high so that population numbers are just about static: **Fogo, Cape Verde Islands**

Counterurbanisation in remoter areas, largely retirement and teleworking: North Yorkshire, **California**

Counterurbanisation in the accessible Midlands and **Oxfordshire**

In developing areas, the trend of rural–urban migration began much later, in the 1950s in South America and from the 1970s in Asia and Africa. There were strong disparities in opportunity between the poverty-stricken rural areas (issues of a lack of employment and basic health and education services, as well as uncertainties caused by natural disasters such as drought-related famines). Subsequently the growing large urban areas were seen as having better services and employment prospects. In general it was those aged between 16 and 40, especially males, who migrated, often to the nearest large town, before sometimes moving on to very large cities (a process known as step-migration).

In general birth rates were traditionally very high in rural areas (c. 3%), so the out-migration rarely led to extreme rural depopulation, although it did cause difficulties in farming the land to provide food, which became the role of the elderly, especially women. Where HIV/AIDS was prevalent, however, or extreme famines or wars had occurred, many children and babies died, so rural depopulation became apparent. There are a number of factors which tend to stem the flow of out-migration, as the case study of Burkina Faso shows (*Case study 12*). These include successful rural development (often by NGOs) and schemes funded by remittances sent back by successful migrants. The Vietnamese case study (*Case study 11*) also shows how government-funded and organised schemes to eradicate rural poverty can also begin to stabilise the situation.

In some developing countries, especially in South America, and to some extent in South Africa, counterurbanisation is just beginning, as rich urban dwellers seek to build their luxury homes in the **rural–urban fringe** zone and commute to work, or in the case of China rural land is 'grabbed' to develop new urban settlements.

Figure 2.3
Population change in rural areas in developing countries

Figure 2.3 summarises the impacts of demographics and migration flows on the structure of population in developing areas.

In developed areas traditionally high birth rates

Rural development schemes — both government and NGO

Impact of HIV/AIDS leads to many deaths, slows birth rate

Rural revival
Population continues to rise but at a less rapid rate as opportunities arise; flow is stemmed by rural development schemes

+

Static

−

Rural depopulation
In rare areas often affected by AIDS and famine

Some trickle-back where rural development schemes

Small flows of successful migrants back to country

Out-migration of 16–40-year-olds

Urban area

Shanty towns

While the predominant movement is currently out-migration, the populations are in general growing but at differential rates, as illustrated by the case studies.

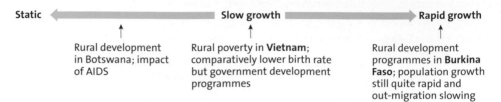

Static	Slow growth	Rapid growth
Rural development in Botswana; impact of AIDS	Rural poverty in **Vietnam**; comparatively lower birth rate but government development programmes	Rural development programmes in **Burkina Faso**; population growth still quite rapid and out-migration slowing

Changes in the developed world: population and services

Figure 2.4 summarises the vicious cycle of depopulation. Absolute depopulation is likely to occur if people leave and are not replaced. Examples exist of deserted villages in the Apennines and the Spanish Meseta, and in rural Japan (*Case study 4*). A threshold of non-viability is reached (a tipping point), where it becomes uneconomic to supply private or public services, leading to accelerating decline.

Relative depopulation occurs where young people leave but are replaced by, for example, retired people. In this case, while population numbers remain similar, the ageing society will ultimately contribute to a state of natural decrease (hence the forecasts in the Japan case study). Moreover, second-homers also purchase much of the property in attractive coastal or remote villages, again contributing to depopulation by forcing house prices beyond the reach of local people. Figure 2.4

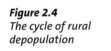

Figure 2.4
The cycle of rural depopulation

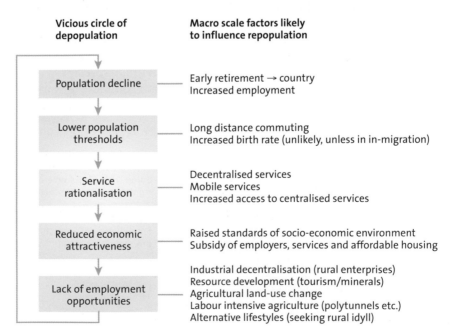

Vicious circle of depopulation

- Population decline
- Lower population thresholds
- Service rationalisation
- Reduced economic attractiveness
- Lack of employment opportunities

Macro scale factors likely to influence repopulation

Early retirement → country
Increased employment

Long distance commuting
Increased birth rate (unlikely, unless in in-migration)

Decentralised services
Mobile services
Increased access to centralised services

Raised standards of socio-economic environment
Subsidy of employers, services and affordable housing

Industrial decentralisation (rural enterprises)
Resource development (tourism/minerals)
Agricultural land-use change
Labour intensive agriculture (polytunnels etc.)
Alternative lifestyles (seeking rural idyll)

shows the macro-scale factors likely to stem depopulation or even encourage repopulation. The experience of the USA (*Case study 5*) shows that even where the situation was thought to be beyond redemption, the macro-factors of worldwide recession in 2008–10 actually led to a revival of some areas in the Dakotas such as Sioux City, as these places were relatively untouched by the credit crunch.

The Isle of Harris in the Outer Hebrides is seeking to rebrand the whole island as Scotland's third national park in order to address its absolute decline in population (see *Case study 18*).

The case study of Fogo in the Cape Verde Islands (*Case study 6*) shows a declining community whose numerical loss is masked by a continuing high birth rate. Tthe Cape Verde Islands, a former Portuguese possession, are in some ways a developing country, but have the fourth highest per capita GNP in Africa. With measures in place to stem the outflow of young people, such as providing further education and upgrading the infrastructure, the situation is potentially reversible.

THE ENDANGERED COMMUNITIES OF JAPAN

Case study 4

As a result of Japan's rapidly ageing and overall decreasing population (Japan has never had strong pro-natalist strategies or encouraged widespread immigration), communities deep within the mountainous areas are finding it increasingly difficult to survive: 2643 communities are likely to disappear in the future and 423 are in danger of disappearing within a decade. Since the last survey in 1999, 191 communities have completely vanished.

Residents of these ageing and rapidly shrinking communities face numerous difficulties. Bus services are being abandoned because of lack of users, community events are being discontinued because of lack of participants, and elderly residents spend thousands of yen getting to hospital appointments — these communities are endangered because all their social functions disintegrate. Diminishing communities also adversely affect the surrounding ecosystems and other communities downstream from the mountains, because of the lack of people to farm the land. Abandoned rice

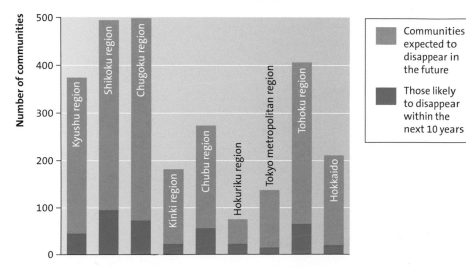

Figure 2.5
The number of communities on the brink of disappearing in Japan, April 2006

paddies have an impact on the firefly and frog population, and woods not managed and appropriately thinned lose their capability to retain water.

The biggest issue is whether local governments can support these shrinking, sparsely populated communities, and how.

One suggestion is to relocate the few remaining elderly people to more convenient areas, to cut administrative costs, and so to abandon these marginal areas. Some local governments have launched schemes to attract migrants from urban areas with subsidies, or to develop innovative ways of providing services and also to support farmers who are cultivating the steep slopes in the endangered communities, but the future is very gloomy for remote rural Japan.

Case study 5 THE PLAINS DRAIN IN THE USA

Figure 2.6 locates the key areas of rural depopulation in the USA — note the huge swathe of country stretching through middle America. Eleven states cover around 15% of the US land area and are all facing depopulation and rural decline in many counties.

North Dakota is one of the most sparsely populated states in the USA (average population density 3.6 per km^2). Overall the state has a static population fluctuating around the 650 000 mark, but some of its most rural counties, e.g. Hettinger, have experienced depopulation of up to 50% in the last 20 years. Most out-migrants are young adults aged between 20 and 35 and they migrate to the only two towns, Bismark (100 000 — capital) and Fargo (200 000 — main town), and the large cities such as Minneapolis. This leaves behind a greater proportion of older people, leading to an ageing population and the potential for natural population decrease (Figure 2.7). A plethora of issues including shortage of jobs, a harsh climate (especially in winter) and isolation from comforts and services combine as push factors.

Figure 2.6
Rural depopulation in the USA

Contemporary Case Studies

The decline in population means that some businesses and services are forced to close, leading to a spiral of decline. Falling population also means a declining local tax base and an inability to provide public services (schools etc.) and infrastructure. The population of Mott, the principal urban centre of Hettinger, declined from a high of 1600 in 1950 to 800 in 2000. In 1950 there were over 80 businesses, but now only a handful remain, and the high school, even after a merger with a school in a neighbouring county, only has under 70 students today. Following the US subprime mortgage crisis, many homes remain empty.

In Cheyenne County in eastern Colorado circumstances are a little different — the current record prices for wheat and the growth of corn for biofuels mean it is not especially poor. The root problem is a shrinking agricultural employment base. Improvements in technology favour huge, highly mechanised farms, and as farmers retire or quit, their land is bought by huge agribusinesses. In 2006 this small county lost 300 people in just one year, so depopulation is again an accelerating process as services close. Three hopes for survival include windfarms, superfast internet and a superhighway from Mexico to Canada which could pass through Cheyenne county.

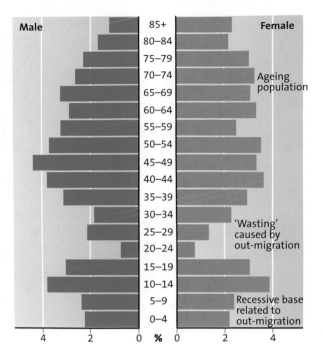

Figure 2.7
Population pyramid for Hettinger County in 2002

The challenge for the future in the Prairies and the Plains is not to stem the tide (deemed impossible) but to keep life as pleasant as possible for those who remain. To young people in particular these areas seem very unequal spaces, with major issues of opportunity deprivation and mobility deprivation exacerbated by rising fuel costs.

FOGO, CAPE VERDE ISLANDS

Case study **6**

In spite of a comparatively high birth rate among a young, fertile population, which means that overall the total population remains static at around 38 000, the island registered a net loss of over 6600 people over the last 10 years, i.e. around 16% of the total.

The out-migration is largely to Praia on Santiago Island, especially by the younger people in search of training. In the 1940s, the population of Fogo actively decreased as there was so much out-migration to the Boston area of the USA and to Fortaleza in Brazil. Push factors included a lack of infrastructure (only 44% of households had electricity and only 30% had running water; 71% dumped garbage outside their houses) and a lack of employment, with a diminishing tourist industry, fluctuating agriculture and limited manufacturing — in 2000 unemployment rates were over 30%.

Forty-two per cent of Fogo's population were registered as poor, with many families relying on remittances from abroad to survive. Housing surveys suggested that only 56% had a bathroom with toilet, and only 7% owned a truck or car. Furthermore, 36% of families were receiving insufficient food. All these facts suggest that poverty is at the

Figure 2.8
Poor living conditions on Fogo, Cape Verde Islands

root of out-migration. The only reason why there is currently not an overall decline in Fogo's population is the consistently high rate of natural increase. While Cape Verde is considered to be Africa's fourth wealthiest state, inequality of opportunity and wealth between the islands is what drives the out-migration (Figure 2.8).

Counterurbanisation and the rural turnaround

Figure 2.9
Predominance of counterurbanisation and urbanisation for 11 European countries

Counterurbanisation is almost entirely a phenomenon of the developed world, although the twenty-first century has seen it begin in Chile, Argentina and Brazil. Figure 2.9 shows how it varies (spatially) over time in a range of countries.

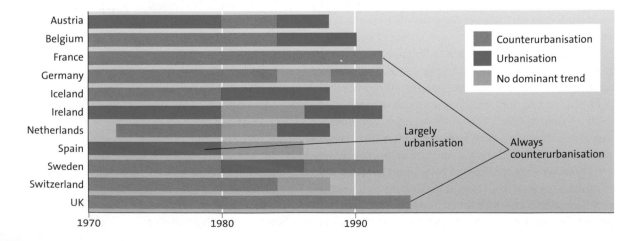

Contemporary Case Studies

As counterurbanisation is technically defined as 'the increase in the proportion of people living in areas defined as rural in a country or region', it involves not only urban-to-rural migration but also an element of natural increase that can result if the productive element of the population migrate — i.e. commuters, who are in the 25–50 age range and who may take children with them or enlarge their families. In some rural areas this movement has resulted in population growth for the first time in decades — for example in Robin Hood's Bay, North Yorkshire, where the broadband revolution drew enough young families to provide a critical mass to save the village school. Sometimes the development of a sustainable community can attract key middle-class professionals to form a nucleus of incomers. The key factors driving counterurbanisation are:

- economic cyclical factors that encourage periods of rural investment and enterprise development
- economic structural factors that cause the decentralisation of jobs to rural areas, leading to better rural employment opportunities
- spatial and environmental factors such as issues of congestion, pollution and crime in urban areas, housing availability and costs, and quality of rural environmental amenities
- socio-economic and socio-cultural factors, including changing demographic composition (e.g. an ageing society seeking retirement in the countryside)
- government policies, including explicit initiatives to promote rural development such as innovative schemes to improve rural services or to attract migrants
- technological innovations, including improved transport links for commuting, and telecommunications (broadband revolution)
- aspirational migration — the perception of a rural idyll and a place in the country that can provide a better lifestyle

Note how the circumstances can change — for example, city centre regeneration, declining rural services and the economic and social costs of commuting are driving many people back to city living (reurbanisation).

The following case studies of California and west Oxfordshire show how counter-urbanisation rates can vary significantly, both spatially and temporally.

COUNTERURBANISATION IN CALIFORNIA

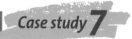

Case study **7**

Figure 2.10 shows the areas experiencing counterurbanisation in California.

Initially, flows from the 1960s followed major roads as people moved out of Los Angeles, San Francisco and San Diego to accessible rural areas such as Orange County, Santa Clara and Escondido respectively. Many of these migrants were professionals who commuted to work along the freeways. In time so-called **edge cities** were built, such as Irvine in Orange County, where a huge range of high-tech and quaternary employment developed. Growth is still very apparent, but at a slower rate than in the 1970s and 1980s. Other suburbs of Los Angeles, such as Riverside, are now faster-growing, with 30% increases recorded since 1990s. The growth of Silicon Valley south of San Francisco is a parallel development leading to huge growth around San José.

In the 1980s and 1990s a second strand of migration developed. This was largely amenity or aspirational migration, to areas such as Lake Tahoe, Mammoth Lakes and

Figure 2.10
Counterurbanisation in California

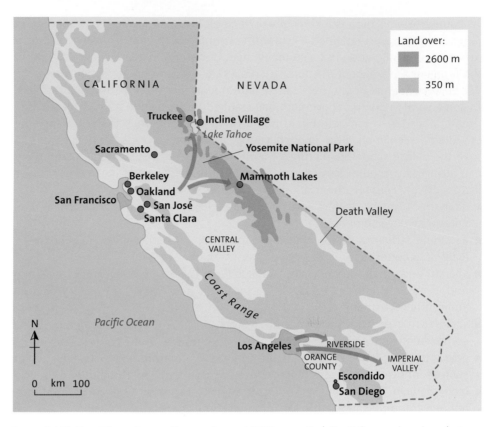

Imperial Valley. These have all experienced 30% growth (albeit from a low base) since the 1990s. A common pattern was for people aged 40-plus living in the big cities to purchase a holiday home, either for vacation or as an investment unit to rent with the ultimate aim of using it for retirement. These people sought to locate in areas of high environmental quality, with access to recreational opportunities such as fishing or trekking, in an area of low crime and high tranquillity. They were able to remortgage or sell their high-value suburban properties to purchase attractive homes on readily available plots in private land areas not protected by federal or state governments.

Although the Lake Tahoe shoreline is now very highly priced, other areas such as Truckee are relatively affordable compared with Incline Village, and therefore are inhabited by a different age group (largely 20 to 45) drawn to a Sierra Nevada lifestyle and opportunities for employment in tourism or other service industries. In Mammoth Lakes, house prices are even higher (median around $1 million in 2007 — before the recession), largely because of the influx of middle-class professionals who telecommute.

Imperial Valley is a much less expensive county and also less homogeneous, with large numbers of Hispanic Americans. It does, however, provide an attractive climate and a more rural location for many former suburban residents of Los Angeles, and also for many Canadians. In all these areas as the resident populations grow above the critical threshold there are many benefits such as the development of a range of high-order services, which make for very convenient living (such as hospitals, schools, dentists etc.). The services are partly sustained by year-round tourism, especially at Lake Tahoe, which can triple the population.

There are inevitably environmental issues, such as the physical sprawl of low-density settlements up the mountain sides, and the potential problem of pollution of lakes and rivers, although the latter is currently managed. Moreover, counterurbanisation and the demand for second homes (around 40% in both Lake Tahoe and Mammoth Lakes but only 15% in Imperial Valley) have led to escalation in house prices, taking them beyond the reach of local people.

COUNTERURBANISATION IN WEST OXFORDSHIRE

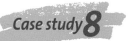

Case study 8

West Oxfordshire has a population of over 100 000 people, most of whom live in market towns and larger villages. Witney is the largest settlement, a market town home to over 25 000 people. While west Oxfordshire is rural, it is very much an accessible rural area, within commuting distance of a number of large urban areas such as Swindon and Oxford. The most accessible rural villages and towns have grown the most, but the overall population has increased by over 25% since 1981.

Figure 2.11 shows the variety of settlements within this comparatively small area. The *West Oxfordshire Settlement Sustainability Report* has classified the 120 settlements by size, character and role, in particular the number of services and facilities offered. The present housing stock in west Oxfordshire is estimated to be just under 40 000 units.

Figure 2.11
Counterurbanisation in west Oxfordshire

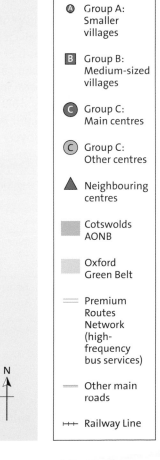

The Oxfordshire Structure Plan requires west Oxfordshire to develop 6750 individual units by 2011 (again envisaging another 25% increase in population). The report emphasised the need to steer the majority of these increases to the larger settlements, which provide a wide range of existing facilities and services, a local employment base and a reasonable level of public transport provision. It also emphasised the need to locate new housing where it will have the least adverse impact on the character and resources of west Oxfordshire. In many of the smaller villages there are a number of physical constraints, such as designation as part of the Cotswolds AONB or other conservation area, or remoteness from a principal road that would increase local traffic congestion on the rural roads, as well as the lack of basic services, which would further add to car use. In spite of this it is only planning controls that are limiting the growth of these villages.

Additionally, the new residential accommodation has to provide a variety of sizes, types and affordability. The main socio-economic features of west Oxfordshire currently include:

■ high levels of home ownership — only 13% of housing is for rent from housing associations
■ high levels of highly priced detached properties
■ high levels of professional and managerial occupations
■ high levels of car ownership and car use (70% use for work)
■ high levels of community mobility, with many newcomers

In general there is strong local opposition to expansion of many of these Oxfordshire villages, as counterurbanisation on a large scale or at an accelerated pace may lead to loss of village character, as shown in Table 2.1 below. The high-profile, well-orchestrated campaign (the Weston Front) against the proposed eco-town at Weston Otmoor is an example of this (*Case study 23*).

Hudson's model of a suburbanised village, showing ribbon development along roads, infill, modifications of existing properties (accretions) and adjuncts of modern estates is very applicable to many of the larger west Oxfordshire villages (Figure 2.12).

Table 2.1
The effects of counterurbanisation on village character

Characteristics	Original village	Suburban village
Housing	Stone-built houses with slate or thatch roof, some farms, barns, most over 100 years old; distinctive vernacular architecture	New, mainly detached houses on small estates, renovated gentrified cottages, barn conversions, double garages
Inhabitants	Primary jobs such as farming, crafts, labouring and manual jobs; work locally	Professionals, executives, commuters, often wealthy middle-class families or retired; some new rural businesses
Transport	Rural bus service, narrow winding road network, limited cars	Declining bus service until recent plans as most families have at least two cars; improved roads, but some congestion
Services	Village shop, small junior school, pub, village hall, blacksmith, baker, butcher	Closure of basic shops, some new specialised shops, modern gastro pubs, enlarged school
Social	Small, close-knit community	Local community may be swamped, village may be deserted by day — 'ghost town'
Environment	Quiet, relatively pollution-free, village green, open spaces	More noise and risk of more pollution, loss of farmland

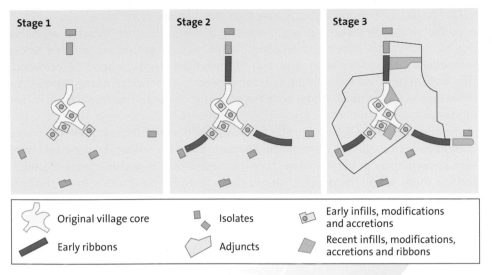

Figure 2.12
Hudson's model of a suburbanised village

Stage 1

Stage 2

Stage 3

Original village core	Isolates	Early infills, modifications and accretions
Early ribbons	Adjuncts	Recent infills, modifications, accretions and ribbons

MIGRATION WORKERS IN RURAL AREAS

Case study **9**

While the more rapid growth in rural population is almost totally driven by counterurbanisation, and the overall numbers of eastern European migrants who have registered for work in rural areas is by comparison small (120 000 between 2004 and 2006), locally, their migration has had major impacts on rural areas because of its marked concentrations. It can lead to localised population growth, as in Boston, which in 2009 had the highest fertility rate in the UK.

Major concentrations are shown in Figure 2.13. The highest concentration of all is in Boston, Lincolnshire, where nearly 20% of the workforce was born in **A8** countries. While overall 62% of all A8 migrants were Poles, the highest percentage of the labour force (around 10%) actually migrated from Lithuania, followed by Latvia. Another feature is the concentrations by nationality.

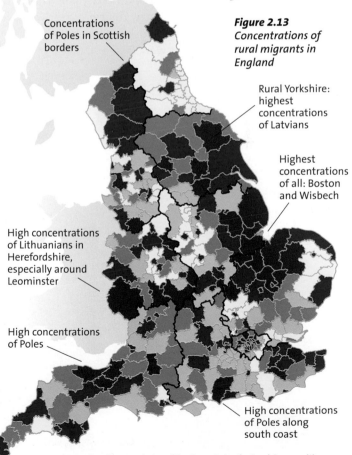

Figure 2.13
Concentrations of rural migrants in England

Concentrations of Poles in Scottish borders

Rural Yorkshire: highest concentrations of Latvians

Highest concentrations of all: Boston and Wisbech

High concentrations of Lithuanians in Herefordshire, especially around Leominster

High concentrations of Poles

High concentrations of Poles along south coast

Reproduced by permission of the Commission for Rural Communities

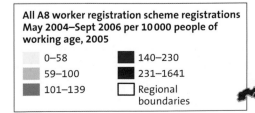

All A8 worker registration scheme registrations May 2004–Sept 2006 per 10 000 people of working age, 2005

0–58	140–230
59–100	231–1641
101–139	Regional boundaries

The attraction to rural areas is based on the availability of work (33% work in manufacturing such as fish and food processing, 25% in agriculture, fruit and vegetable picking, and 20% in hotels and retailing). While many migrants are working below their educational qualification level, and for minimum wages (around £6 per hour), they have established a reputation as reliable, industrious workers. Many, if they stay, move up the occupational ladder once fluent in English, and some fill skills shortages (doctors, dentists, plumbers).

The migrants have a different profile from the British population in that they are more likely to be male, single and without dependants. In host areas, often small market towns such as Leominster in Herefordshire, they therefore form a very visible presence, especially in shops where there are Polish or eastern European food aisles, in overflowing Catholic churches, or in pubs and cafés and talking in foreign languages in the streets. Inevitably tensions spill over, often fuelled by misconception and rumour, as rural areas have had little experience of 'foreigners' and some of the indigenous population are xenophobic (evidence of anti-Polish graffiti), especially as it is wrongly perceived that immigrants are taking British jobs and soaking up British benefits. The reality, as a Herefordshire survey showed in 2006, is that the migrants contributed more to GDP per capita than their number would suggest, although inevitably they send back large amounts in remittances. Only 6% bring dependants (spouse and children) with them. They do, however, occupy jobs in the unskilled sector, making it difficult for poorly qualified 'early entry' 16-year-old school leavers to get jobs, especially in periods of recession.

In Herefordshire, the migration shows definite seasonality, as so many of the migrants work for S & A, the largest strawberry agribusiness in the UK, under the SAWS

Figure 2.14
Migrant workers picking commercially farmed daffodils in northeast Scotland

Shenval/Alamy

(Seasonal Agricultural Workers Scheme). Locals are very aware of the convoys of green buses taking them to work from their huge mobile home parks. A recent planning enquiry turned down the development of a permanent migrant village (for up to 5000 eastern Europeans) combined with extension of poly tunnels (visual eyesores). A second modified version is being submitted, based on the concept of tabletop growth of strawberries and diminishing amounts of new poly tunnels. Without migrant workers it is doubtful whether agribusinesses could survive.

Although the scale and pace of eastern European migration have caused concern, especially as locally it puts pressure on key services (health and education), there is evidence that it is an example of **churning**, with up to 40% change each year. Increasingly Poles are returning home, as unemployment in the UK has soared and the Polish economy has performed relatively well. Moreover, the devaluation of the pound against the euro has meant that the wages paid to the migrants are now worth much less, as many currencies such as the Polish zloty are to some extent tied to the euro.

The issue is that many agricultural enterprises cannot do without migrant labour. Parallels can be drawn with the USA (Mexican migrants), Germany (Kosovans), Spain (Moroccans) and Italy (Romanians). As the Poles return, new sources of supply from Romania and Bulgaria (newly admitted to the EU) are sought, although in this case there are restrictions on numbers until 2014.

For many migrants, living and working in areas as beautiful as Hereford, Shetland, the Scottish Highlands or the Cambridgeshire Fens has been an excellent experience, but on the other hand some migrants have experienced cramped housing conditions, minimal wages, and exploitation by gang masters who first recruited them. They have also experienced language difficulties, above average rates of unemployment, and in some cases outright hostility from local communities, possibly inspired by anti-Polish sentiments regularly expressed by the popular press.

The question to consider is: will there be a lasting impact on the rural communities they lived and worked in?

---

4 **Using case studies**

Using a quadrant form (see example), evaluate the positives and negatives of A8 migration to rural areas.

	Host	Source
+		
−		

Changing services

Theoretically there should be a direct link between population and services: more people should lead to more services, and vice versa. The reality, however, is far more complex as it varies between countries, and according to whether the rural settlements are located in remote, accessible or rural–urban fringe areas.

Services have traditionally been provided either by governments (i.e. public services) or by commercial providers (private services), although in the light of the need to develop innovative solutions, many of the latest ideas on provision favour public–private partnerships. Services provided by governments are influenced by availability of funding. In an era of increasing accountability and cost-awareness both national and local governments need to rationalise services in order to control or even cut costs. They tend to close services in areas of higher population density, where alternatives exist, but in remote areas they pursue strategies which consolidate a range of core services (school, post office etc.) in key settlements to ensure that all people are within a reasonable distance of provision. This may even mean that uneconomic services such as village schools with only 6–10 children are kept open. Private services such as general stores, garages or petrol stations are run for profit motives, so they need to be commercially viable as businesses.

Therefore in the UK, while in general rural populations are increasing, trade at village businesses is not, as increasing car ownership and even free supermarket buses mean that people prefer a trip to the supermarket for food and petrol (where choice is greater and prices are generally lower) either in nearby market towns or out-of-town retail parks.

Table 2.2 summarises the changing services situation in the UK between 1991 and 2000.

Table 2.2
The changing services situation in the UK between 1991 and 2000 (percentage of villages)

Worsening situation compared with 1991	Apparently stable situation	Improving situation compared with 1991
Permanent shop (42%) Post office (43%) Seven-day bus service (75%) Bank or building society (91%) Police station (92%)	Pub (29%), especially in tourist areas Petrol station (65%), many diversified GP surgery (95%), very low base	Village hall or similar (32%) Bottle bank/recycling (60%) Community minibus or social car scheme (79%) Public or private nursery (96%) Day care for elderly (91%)

Source: Rural Services Survey, Countryside Agency, 2000

The situation 10 years later in 2010 is very mixed. While there have been new initiatives from the government, such as the extended schools project, and the use of Millennium Grants to fund village halls — new multi-purpose community resource centres — in general the situation has become worse in many villages. For instance, in Somerset, services have increased in the market town of Crewkerne but have declined in nearly all the 17 villages in the catchment area (especially those that are not on main roads).

- Schools are seen as the lifeblood of any village — they ensure that young families with children are attracted as in-migrants. Counties such as Staffordshire and Herefordshire (in 2008–09) have established cost-cutting strategies to shut and amalgamate rural primary schools. This has aroused huge opposition, as many of them have around 70 pupils and are in thriving villages. This is not strictly government policy, but it reflects the problems local councils are experiencing in providing schools and other services.

- Doctors' surgeries are vital for village life, especially for those ageing communities which are so common in areas such as Cornwall. Government policy has been to promote, via the Primary Care Trusts, larger polyclinic surgeries, as these can to some extent replace the closed cottage hospitals and are seen as more efficient. The downside is that many rural practices are one- or two-doctor practices that struggle to access the various incentive payments. If these shut, the elderly and sick are forced to travel longer distances for treatment and they often lack access to a car or a rural bus service that can connect them to their appointment (and return them).

- The big issue of 2009 was the closure of post offices, again vital to village life as they are combined with a village store and provide basic essentials for villagers. As the government has shifted many post office services to private contractors and pushed some dealings online (e.g. for car tax renewal), many post offices have become marginal in terms of profit, with Royal Mail running up such a huge deficit that rationalisation of post offices, including many suburban and rural offices, has become vital.

- Pubs are also closing, at the rate of at least one per day (2009) — again the lifeblood of a village for entertainment and community interaction. Here the reasons for closure are complex, ranging from the credit crunch (people eating out less) and the smoking ban to 'overgreedy' breweries that own chains of pubs and need to maximise profits.

- Garages and petrol stations have also closed, especially those that are away from main roads, as they cannot buy petrol to sell at the same prices as the supermarkets. In rural Northumberland this has become a particular issue, as many people are 20 km from a fill-up.

Sue Warn

Figure 2.15
Rural services under threat: 'Save our school' — schools are seen as the lifeblood of any village; private services such as post offices/general stores, garages/petrol stations need to be commercially viable as businesses

A 2009 survey estimated that in the following year 600 pubs and 400 village shops would close. The root cause was identified as the lack of affordable housing, which was pushing young rural families away from villages, so sucking the life out of these settlements.

Table 2.3 summarises the current situation in terms of access to services in south Shropshire, one of the most remote districts in England. There is considerable incidence of opportunity deprivation, especially for the very young and the elderly (fourth-agers who are 75-plus), who experience mobility deprivation as they have to rely on public transport. Figure 2.16 shows those who are suffering as a result of declining services.

Table 2.3 *Percentage access to services in south Shropshire*

Service	Within 2 km	Between 3–9 km	Over 10 km	Change
Bank	56.2	35.8	8.0	—
Cash point	65.4	34.4	0.2	—
Doctors' surgery	63.8	35.9	0.3	—
Job centre	0	2.0	98.0	—
Public house	82.0	18.0	0	↓
Petrol station	65.4	33.4	1.2	↓
Post office	75.7	24.1	0.2	↓
Primary school	78.7	21.1	0.2	↓
Secondary school	44.9	38.2	16.9	—
Supermarket	41.8	30.7	27.5	—

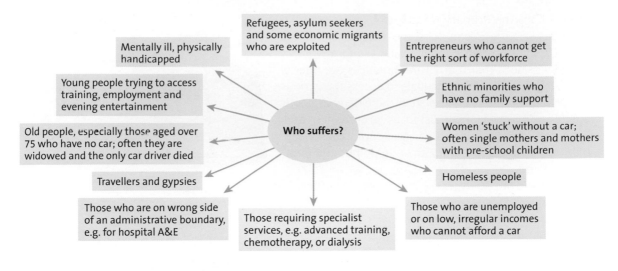

Figure 2.16
*Who suffers from
declining services in
rural areas?*

The situation in France is much better than in the UK, as traditionally the French have favoured local services (think about fresh baguettes from the village baker). Even where depopulation has occurred, as in rural Brittany (*Case study 2*), services remain supported by the local *communes*, which raise taxes to keep them open.

The situation in the USA is a closer parallel to that in the UK. In areas of rural depopulation (*Case study 5*) there has been a huge decline in services, but in areas where tourism has 'taken off', e.g. Mammoth Lakes in California (see *Case study 7*), services have expanded and also changed to reflect the growing population of commuters and teleworkers, all of whom demand greater diversity of services.

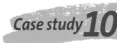

THE IMPACT OF TOURISM ON SERVICES

- Tourism, especially when it is year-round, can directly add both numbers and volume of sales, thus increasing the range, size and viability of local businesses and services such as general stores, pubs and restaurants, which the local community uses.
- Tourists can also contribute to, and improve, the social and community life of settlements, for example by taking part in local events and festivals; the money raised often goes back into local charities and the community.
- Tourism can lead to improvements in infrastructure, for example roads, and it can also add improvements to the built environment by taking over derelict buildings and brownfield sites.

These positive benefits in terms of services are of course often outweighed by the costs of tourism, especially if the flows are badly managed.

Indirectly tourism can put money into residents' pockets, creating a positive multiplier effect whereby they can feed money back into the local community.

Rothbury (population 2600) is an unspoilt small market town in a remote, rural part of Northumberland. It is an important local centre whose catchment area has suffered some depopulation, but the town itself has grown steadily, as it is attractive to commuters and even more so to retired people, many of whom were formerly professional workers and have comfortable retirement incomes.

Figure 2.17
Rothbury

Rothbury has nearly 40 shops and 15 cafés and restaurants, as well as services such as primary and middle schools, police, fire and ambulance services, two banks and many leisure facilities. This is significantly above average for its size. Tourism has undoubtedly enhanced businesses such as upmarket clothes and shoe shops. There is also a very fine art gallery for Coquetdale amateur painters, housed in a former industrial building.

5

Using case studies

Figure 2.18 *Summary of changing services across the spectrum in developed countries*

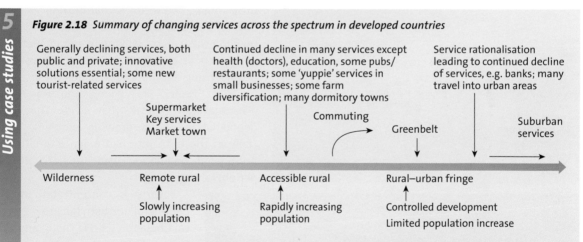

Study Figure 2.18 and carry out the following fieldwork for a village known to you:
(a) Map the businesses and services currently located there.
(b) Use questionnaire techniques to find out how far people have to travel for services not in the village.
(c) Use a combination of old maps, interviews with elderly people, and old directories to see how services have changed since 1970.
(d) Use the census (www.statistics.gov.uk) to find out how the population in your village has changed (by numbers and structure).
(e) To what extent does your village fit the model for a remote, accessible or rural–urban fringe village?

Changes in the developing world: population and services

Figure 2.19
Map showing the location of Vietnam's northern hill provinces

In many countries in the developing world, traditional rural societies dependent on subsistence agriculture dominate, especially in the peripheral regions. For example in Vietnam, a newly industrialised country in southeast Asia, the proportion of households living below the poverty line has fallen — from 60% in 1993 to around 25% in 2008. Until recently most economic development has been in southern Vietnam, particularly in Ho Chi Minh City (HMC), which is seen as a very attractive environment for foreign direct investment. At the same time, most of the new jobs created in manufacturing, tourism and other service industries have been on the coast and in urban areas. The result is that in rural Vietnam poverty levels have improved (trickle-down), but nowhere near as rapidly as in urban Vietnam, which acts as a magnet for young, enterprising people living in the countryside: these move to HMC, Hanoi, Hai Phong and Da Nang, accentuating the rural–urban divide. Thus rural depopulation was a growing problem, especially as the birth rate had fallen dramatically. An ageing population was apparent in the peripheral regions.

Poverty is concentrated in the peripheral northern hill provinces of Lai Chau, Lao Cai, Ha Giang and Cao Bang, where many non-Vietnamese (ethnic) hill tribes live (Figures 2.19 and 2.20).

Vietnam is a Communist state and tends to address issues of poverty and disparity with a **top-down** model, with centralised economic planning as a core strategy (as in earlier Soviet and Chinese models) which provincial governments are required to carry out.

Peter Chambers/Alamy

Figure 2.20 *Terraced rice fields, Lao Cai province, northern Vietnam*

Programme 133	'Hunger Eradication and Poverty Alleviation Programme' 1998–2008 Included extension of credit, resettlement and investment in infrastructure
Programme 135	'Support for the Most Difficult and Remote Communities Programme' Target to reduce 'poor' households from 40% to 25% by 2005. Activities included investment in infrastructure, training and assisted planning
Programmes 327 and 661	'Regreening the Barren Hills' of 1992, replaced in 2000 by the 'Five Million Hectares Programme'. This is a large-scale rural plantation project using irrigation

Table 2.4
Main government initiatives for rural areas

Table 2.4 summarises the main government initiatives for rural areas.

There are a number of reasons for poverty in the upland farming communities, which are shown in Figure 2.21. While poverty alleviation may be constrained by 'one size fits all' top-down planning, the state-sponsored schemes do aim to overcome many key issues.

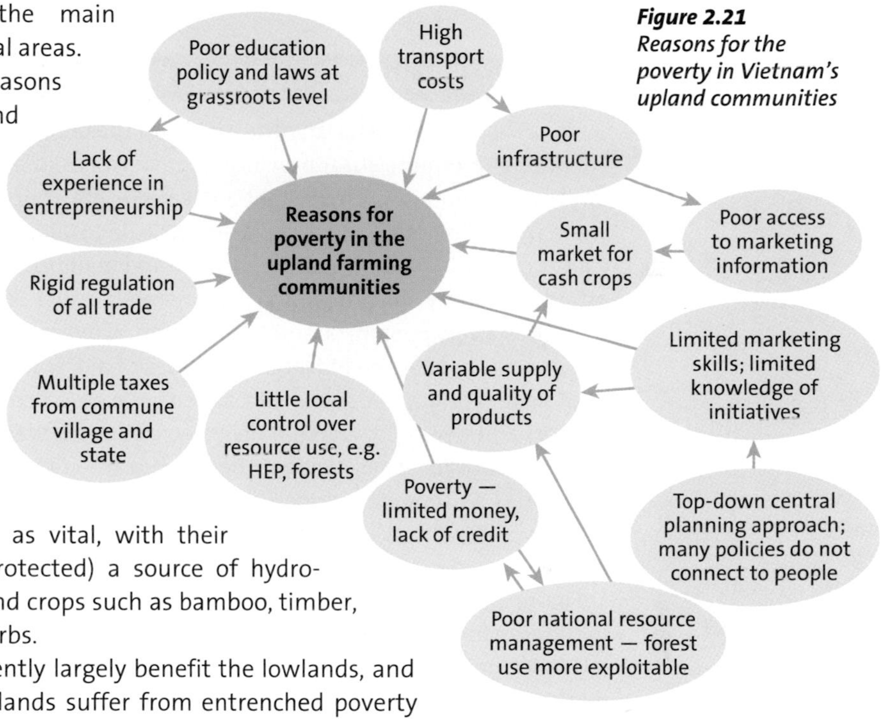

Figure 2.21
Reasons for the poverty in Vietnam's upland communities

Poverty alleviation in the northern uplands

On a national scale these upland regions are regarded as vital, with their forested watersheds (now protected) a source of hydro-electric power (HEP) and upland crops such as bamboo, timber, fruits, spices and medicinal herbs.

However, these goods currently largely benefit the lowlands, and communities living in the uplands suffer from entrenched poverty and even food insecurity, which is especially prevalent among minority ethnic hill tribes. So the potential natural wealth contrasts with the extreme poverty of many communities and families living there.

Vietnam's poorest communities live mainly in upland areas, and the northern mountain region is the poorest area of the country. Over 30% of households in this region are classified as poor (based on per capita income); in some provinces, e.g. Lai Chau, Cao Bang and Ha Giang, the incidence of poverty is as much as 45%.

The government of Vietnam classifies both households and communes by poverty criteria in order to best target delivery of poverty-reducing programmes. Guideline income thresholds are set by central government and can be adjusted by provincial governments. A common measure is to define as poor those with a monthly per capita income of less than 100 000 dong (about $6.50).

Communes are classified as 'poor', and therefore recipients of support under Programme 135, if they satisfy the following six criteria:

■ household income: more than 40% of households are 'poor'
■ isolation: more than 20 km from a centre that has a clinic, school or government office

- infrastructure: lacking roads, electricity, irrigation, clean water supplies
- education: more than 60% of people are illiterate
- agriculture: dependent on forest produce and shifting cultivation
- credit and market access: lacking credit and market access

The official definition of household poverty provides a workable basis for delivering assistance programmes, and the commune-level definition utilises a broader view of poverty, bringing in categories based on local circumstances and opportunities to inform the simple 100 000-dong household income indicator.

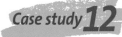

Case study 12 — GNAGNA PROVINCE, BURKINA FASO

Burkina Faso, in sub-Saharan Africa, is one of the poorest countries in the world. Gnagna Province is a remote rural province in eastern Burkina Faso which experiences harsh physical conditions, with drought an ever-present concern, and traditionally very poor standards of health (infant mortality 127 per 1000; life expectancy 44 years; main causes of death: malaria, diarrhoea, polio and malnutrition) and education (only 5% can afford secondary education, and literacy levels are at 26%). Additionally, until recently there was a very poor infrastructure in terms of availability of safe water and electricity. Gnagna has been receiving large quantities of aid. Some prestigious top-down projects such as a World Bank-sponsored agricultural research centre that did little for local farmers and a water tower that delivered clean safe water but at very high cost, proved inappropriate for local needs. Other European NGO projects ran into administrative difficulties as they lacked local knowledge, and the costs of some excellent projects such as a new market were ten times higher than necessary. The main provider of **bottom-up** aid is ASAP (the Association for Promotion of Self Help).

Figure 2.22 summarises the work of ASAP, a low-budget NGO which has been working in the area for nearly 15 years. Its motto is 'Teaching people to fly with their own wings'. It was formed by a group of local people and works especially with women, children and disabled people in remote rural areas.

Figure 2.22
The work of ASAP

One of the villages ASAP has worked in is Bilanga-Yanga. The village was given a kick-start in 1964 when the government funded construction of a dam and a small shallow

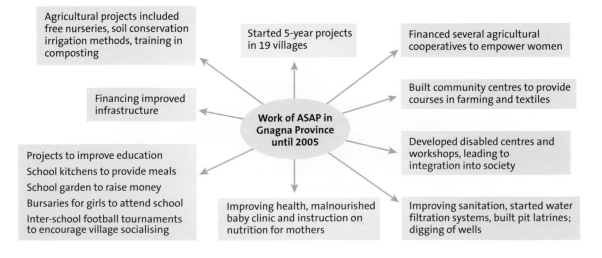

Agricultural projects included free nurseries, soil conservation irrigation methods, training in composting

Started 5-year projects in 19 villages

Financed several agricultural cooperatives to empower women

Financing improved infrastructure

Work of ASAP in Gnagna Province until 2005

Built community centres to provide courses in farming and textiles

Projects to improve education
School kitchens to provide meals
School garden to raise money
Bursaries for girls to attend school
Inter-school football tournaments to encourage village socialising

Developed disabled centres and workshops, leading to integration into society

Improving health, malnourished baby clinic and instruction on nutrition for mothers

Improving sanitation, started water filtration systems, built pit latrines; digging of wells

reservoir, which meant that 20 hectares of land could be irrigated. The land is divided into 80 quarter-hectare plots and is overseen by a local committee. Each family pays a nominal rent for what is in effect an allotment. Failure to cultivate the plot for a year leads to reallocation. Year-round cultivation produces crops of rice, maize, vegetables and fruit that supplement the diet of villagers. Before this development, out-migration of younger males had been widespread, and the population was growing only slowly despite a very high birth rate. Once a European NGO had built a covered market with lock-up shops, ASAP made a lot of very significant improvements, which provided more diverse employment and skills and also improved the quality of life for the villages.

Despite an improvement in communications with the capital, Ouagadougou, the flow of out-migration has been stemmed, with the effect that the population has increased significantly (by around 1600 in only 17 years). As a result of education and health programmes, infant mortality has decreased and life expectancy has increased. All the projects shown are bottom-up initiatives using appropriate (intermediate) technology.

---

6 · **Using case studies**

(a) **Evaluate the advantages and disadvantages of top-down and bottom-up development styles.**

(b) **Summarise the changes that have taken place in Bilanga-Yanga in terms of range of employment and services.**

As income levels rise in developing nations, more services develop. The driving force here is economic development.

■ Governments gradually supply improved health and education services, often aided by NGO schemes.

■ As more microfinance networks emerge, local people are able to start their own small businesses. A multiplier effect develops as income levels increase among local people and the businesses become more viable.

■ In general, population levels have risen (*Case studies 11 and 12*) where either governments or NGOs have invested in villages to provide more facilities and businesses, with the result of increased demand for services.

As in developed countries, the individual location of the village and changes in population and economic activity combine to lead to differential degrees of transformation.

Changing employment

While in developing countries subsistence agriculture is still 'the enduring symbol of rurality', in developed countries the situation is very different, with agriculture-related employment becoming increasingly peripheral.

Before the onset of the postwar productionist revolution in agriculture the normal pattern of rural employment was one of 'jobs for life', usually in the community where people were born — or not more than 5 miles away — with people often working as outdoor manual labourers or hired farm workers, living in a tied cottage in a farming hamlet. With that productionist revolution, however, with its emphasis on enhancing cost-effectiveness through capital-intensive, highly mechanised and increasingly specialised farming concentrated in larger units, the demand for farm workers diminished dramatically. The emphasis is now on skilled, trained workers, who often work as agricultural contractors or as farm managers for corporately owned agribusinesses, or alternatively as part-time seasonal labourers for fruit and vegetable picking — a role increasingly filled by migrant workers (see *Case study 9*).

Rural areas are increasingly attractive, especially those that are accessible to service centres and high-tech businesses in science parks or public sector hubs, such as west Oxfordshire (*Case study 8*). (In the UK today 30% of all manufacturing and business actually takes place in rural areas, especially in accessible rural areas such as Cambridgeshire (Silicon Fen).)

The new professional and managerial posts in these locations are largely taken up by middle-class newcomers who seize the opportunity of living the rural idyll and migrating to live in a village in response to national or regional recruitment. These people are residents of the village but are rarely there, because they commute. The divorce of workplace from home causes interesting social issues. There have also been efforts to develop rural manufacturing — usually in response to government grants for rural areas. In Bishop's Castle there used to be a trouser factory in a rural enterprise park, but even the low wages paid in rural south Shropshire could not compete with the low costs of far eastern factories. Much of the current rural manufacturing is food processing.

Some more jobs are now available, but a higher percentage are low-paid (44%, as against 36% in urban areas). Many of them are low-skilled, part-time, seasonal opportunities, and many are with small businesses employing under 20 people (see the Craven Arms survey in *Case study 30*). It is difficult to get accurate statistics on rural unemployment, as it exists in small pockets.

A major issue is not so much high unemployment as high underemployment, with many workers prevented from achieving work and rewards commensurate with their ability and qualifications. Many workers in remote areas therefore make their living by having several jobs.

Constraints in rural employment include the following:
- Recruitment is even now through informal networks, as jobs are 'given out' by family recommendation.
- Many workers, particularly younger ones, lack access to transport — a Catch-22 situation, as they need a car to get to work but cannot afford one if they have no job.
- Low rates of pay will not cover the costs of childcare or transport, so many people lose money by being employed (a particular problem for women).
- There are major shortages of affordable housing. Tied cottages may be a short-term answer, and cause people to 'stay put' in basic employment.

- There are frequent mismatches between the skills and qualifications of applicants and the limited local opportunities available — for example, in the Lizard Peninsula, Cornwall.
- The availability of low-paid jobs has dried up in many agricultural areas, as these are now taken by EU migrants such as Poles, Lithuanians and Slovaks (see *Case study 9*). This has caused tension in areas such as Lincolnshire and Herefordshire.

Another feature of 'new-style' rural employment is the high percentage of self-employed people, many of whom are telecommuters. Others are farmers' wives running their own **farm diversification** businesses, working from home using a broadband connection. In a survey of the Wintles estate, an experiment in sustainable living in Bishop's Castle, over 80% of the house purchasers were found to be teleworkers — in IT, publishing, marketing etc. — who chose to live there because of the perceived high quality of rural life.

Figure 2.23 summarises the changes in employment in a rural village, reflecting the economic restructuring that has taken place.

The precise mix of rural employment available depends on a number of factors — the history of industrial development in the area, the demographic profile (often an attraction), the structure of the local rural economy and the location of the rural area.

Craven Arms (see *Case study 30*), for example, was an important centre for both roads and railways. As an agricultural centre, much of its industry is food processing and agricultural engineering. It also has a number of small businesses and a full range of retailing outlets such as Tuffin's superstore. Other employment is provided by tourism (Shropshire Hills Discovery Centre, Stokesay Castle etc.).

In developing countries, while the main source of 'employment' continues to be subsistence agriculture, there are nevertheless changes. In Bilanga-Yanga (see *Case study 12*), NGOs have set up a whole range of alternative employment in order to make the community more sustainable and thus slow the flow of out-migration to the shanty towns of Ouagadougou, the capital. In the far east, for example in Vietnam, TNCs have established numerous branch plants or subcontracted factories, drawn by the availability of cheap yet good-quality labour. Various government schemes (see *Case study 11*) have diver sified the rural economy and provided more employment.

In yet other areas tourism is providing increasing diversification, as the following case study of Atata shows.

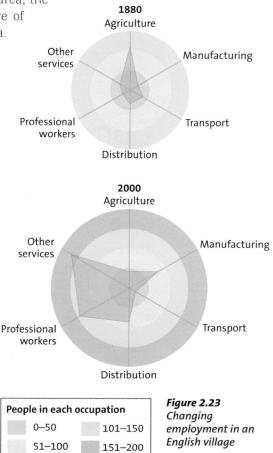

People in each occupation	
0–50	101–150
51–100	151–200

Figure 2.23
Changing employment in an English village

Atata is a small island just 30 minutes by boat from Nuku'alofa, the capital of Tonga, in the south Pacific. As Figure 2.24 shows, there is a symbiotic relationship between the Royal Sunset Hotel and the village. Tourism on small hideaway islands, which unlike the Maldives have working local communities, can create particularly sensitive situations. In this case the construction of the hotel has had beneficial effects on the local community in a number of ways.

Figure 2.24
The impact of tourism on a village community on Atata Island, Tonga

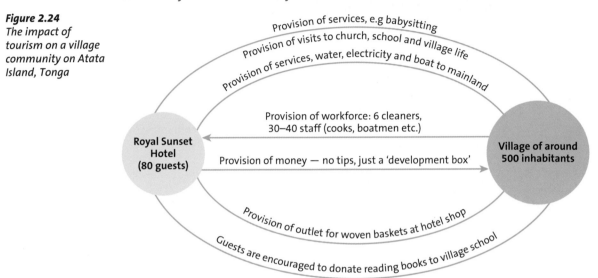

Provision of services, e.g babysitting
Provision of visits to church, school and village life
Provision of services, water, electricity and boat to mainland

Provision of workforce: 6 cleaners, 30–40 staff (cooks, boatmen etc.)

Royal Sunset Hotel (80 guests)

Provision of money — no tips, just a 'development box'

Village of around 500 inhabitants

Provision of outlet for woven baskets at hotel shop
Guests are encouraged to donate reading books to village school

Conclusion

Part 2 has explored changes in population, services and the economy, which have led to a web of interconnected changes in rural areas. The changes have been so profound in developed countries that they have led to the erosion of traditional village communities (Figure 2.25).

The Rural Advocate, when looking at rural communities in England in 2007, identified three groups of communities:

- thriving communities
- fragile communities
- communities dominated by rapid change

Thriving communities are those that have strategies in place to manage the key issues, such as providing affordable housing and a range of key services to ensure a good quality of life for their residents. These communities have a strong and diverse rural economy and a high capacity for community self-help. They have an inbuilt resilience, an ability to weather 'all the storms' and to attract funding for community activities.

Fragile communities are those that have experienced a number of disasters. In the case of UK communities this has included devastation of the farming economy by diseases such as foot and mouth, swine vesicular disease, bird flu and bovine TB. These crippling diseases came to a depressed farm economy — only since about 2007 has there been a revival based on quality of food products, traceability and innovative farm diversification (see page 94). The Cholmondeley Food Hub shows that a fragile farm community can recover. In 2007 and 2008 there were summer floods, especially in the south Midlands, and in 2003 and 2009 farmers faced droughts. However, these disasters have the greatest impact where communities are physically remote. Around 600 000 people live in these very sparse rural areas — for example, Holy Island, which does not even have a cash machine. Even the small settlements in rural Oxfordshire are vulnerable to transport issues. Many of these fragile communities have a high percentage of poverty and disadvantage, with poor access to services and jobs. (Nearly 1 million people live in scattered hidden pockets of poverty — see page 75.) Second homes have also had an impact on these communities, as often the poorest communities, e.g. in Cornwall, have the least affordable housing (ratio of house price to median wage — see page 63). The combined impact of loss of key services, post office, pub, school, shop and petrol station could lead to a tipping point in the erosion of village life.

Changing communities are those experiencing demographic and socio-economic changes, such as the out-migration of young people and the arrival of retired people or migrant workers. There is also the issue of climate change and demands for

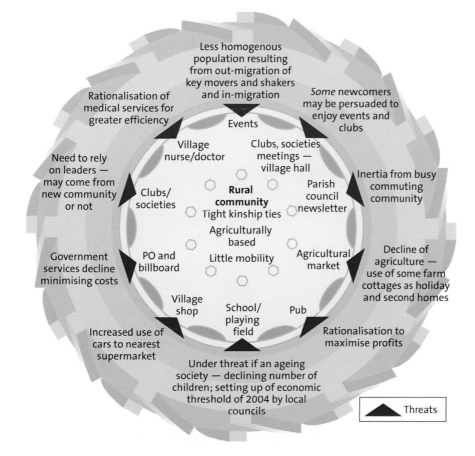

Figure 2.25
The erosion of village communities in developed countries

sustainable energy, which have led to a doubling of the amount of oilseed rape grown, and the arrival of windfarms. Clearly rapid change has the ability to destabilise the community, especially if it is a fragile community. Thriving communities adapt in an innovative way to rapid change and develop sustainable solutions for the future.

This threefold framework is also useful for analysing villages in developing countries. Here thriving communities are those which are supported by successful NGO projects, whereas fragile communities include those badly hit by AIDS, famine or natural disasters. Developing communities are also experiencing rapid change, often associated with new economic developments, which is contributing to the eradication of rural poverty.

Conflicts in the countryside

It is inevitable that changes lead to potential conflicts, especially if they have been rapid and widespread. The socio-cultural and economic restructuring studied in Part 2 has turned rural areas into more complex places with more players contesting the space. However, rural areas are a multifaceted environment potentially capable of accommodating a wide range of uses, provided decision makers take a holistic view of the rural resource base.

In both developed and developing countries the term 'rural' has been very strongly associated with agriculture, whether it be tribal subsistence or family farms and estates. Now pluri-activity is common, with multiple uses.

Competing groups

Conflicts essentially result from the desires of three competing groups:
- farmers and estate owners
- developers
- newcomers

The farmers and estates owners see themselves as the guardians of the country landscape, rural traditional values and communities — a role now enshrined in Europe by EU agricultural reforms which pay farmers to be 'environmental stewards of the land'. Farmers' opinions are diverse. Many farmers see new diversification opportunities as a financial lifeline. Others can unite with newcomers against the threat of development by government that is perceived to be 'urban'.

The developers see rural areas and the countryside as an area of potential for building desirable luxury homes, and business and industrial enterprises. In developed countries, **greenfield sites**, particularly in accessible locations, are seen as ideal locations for depots and service 'farms', as the perceived high quality of the rural environment is a huge marketing bonus. Planning regulations increasingly promote the need for development for economic reasons, at the expense of conservation of the character of rural areas. Only in especially protected areas such as national parks are planning restrictions strong enough to withstand the demands of developers. Current conflicts in the UK include the proposed building of new housing and six

eco-towns, the use of available space for noisy or noxious activities such as waste disposal sites (civic amenity sites), or the expansion of airport runways.

Development of resources is a very controversial topic. Conflicts are numerous and include the use of areas for mining (especially opencast mining), for building energy installations such as windfarms or nuclear power stations, or for commercial logging, all of which have environmental impacts. The first group of case studies looks at resource-based conflicts, especially for energy and water.

Resource-based conflicts also arise with the development of water supply and management. These projects often involve not only the flooding of land for reservoirs but also the building of mega-dams (*Case study 16*) and diversions of increasingly large parts of drainage systems. Conflicts occur not only between developers and conservationists but also between a range of users, especially when the supply of water is finite, as in the Olagalla aquifer in the Great Plains of the USA, which is rapidly diminishing.

The newcomers to the countryside in the developed world are largely middle-class professionals or retired people. Many of this group are anti-development, even though they were part of it, as they see development as destroying their dream of a rural idyll. A particular issue (*Case study 8*) is the provision of housing for these newcomers, as their ability to pay high prices has a huge impact on village life.

While they frequently have very different values from traditional 'country folk' or traditional villagers (over micro-issues such as rural rights of way or farmyard smells, or the right to hunt or to cull badgers), they become the leaders of local NIMBY protests, such as that against the biomass plant in Bishop's Castle (see page 49) or the use of a particular site for a windfarm. These newcomers are often highly organised campaigners, using a wide range of techniques such as websites, e-petitions and lobbying MPs to prevent a particular development.

Figure 3.1
Conflict summary

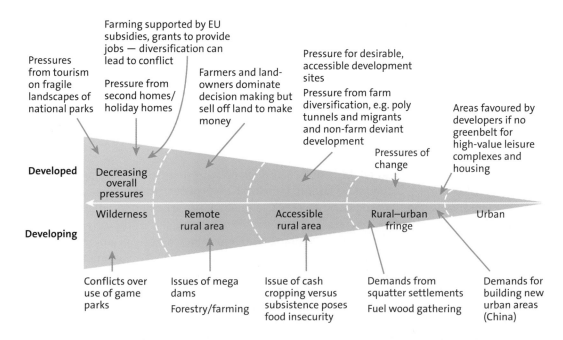

Contemporary Case Studies

In summary, conflicts are about how rural space should be used, by whom and for whom. They can happen at a variety of scales, from a local single-issue protest to a national-scale project such as the 'Liberty and Livelihood' campaign in the UK, initially about the right to hunt but ultimately against the perceived threat from an 'urban' Labour government to the whole fabric of rural life.

As Figure 3.1 shows, the actual balance and focus of conflicts vary across the spectrum of rural environments and between developed and developing countries.

Developing resources for energy, minerals or water in the countryside has proved extremely controversial for two reasons. First, the environmental impact as measured by techniques such as the Leopold matrix is generally very high and rarely compensated for by economic benefits such as creating jobs (as most projects are capital-intensive) and boosting the local economy. Second, the actual resources are often found within areas of outstanding natural beauty or tranquil rural landscapes. The policy decisions made by central governments over future energy mix or water exploitation can have a profound impact on rural areas.

Energy

IMPACTS OF ENERGY DEVELOPMENT ON RURAL BRITAIN

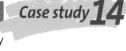

Case study **14**

Developing coal resources has arguably the greatest impact. As aims of energy security are pursued, the role of coal is reviewed, directly in terms of deep mining and opencast developments and indirectly via the building of new thermal coal-fired power stations. While deep mining is unlikely to restart, because in cost terms it fails to compete with lower-priced coal imports, threats of opencast mining can affect many rural areas and people's lives and house prices for many years.

Opencast mining such as that at Butterwell, near Morpeth in Northumberland, where over 13 million tonnes of coal were worked from the 1980s, has a huge local impact, in this case blighting a pleasant area of villages and farms for well over 20 years (original estimate 13 years). Moreover, while the soil is replaced and the land reseeded to 'restore' the ecosystem, research suggests that the actual ecological quality of the hedgerows is far less diverse than that of the originals, and many argue that it takes 50 years for the land to recover.

Figure 3.2 summarises the impacts of the main stages of exploitation.

Figure 3.2
The environmental impacts of opencast mining

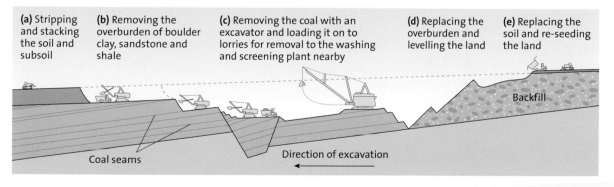

(a) Stripping and stacking the soil and subsoil

(b) Removing the overburden of boulder clay, sandstone and shale

(c) Removing the coal with an excavator and loading it on to lorries for removal to the washing and screening plant nearby

(d) Replacing the overburden and levelling the land

(e) Replacing the soil and re-seeding the land

Backfill

Coal seams

Direction of excavation

There are many rural areas that would be threatened, such as Little Wenlock, Shropshire, which is currently experiencing a planning enquiry for a proposal to extract 900 000 tonnes of coal by opencast mining.

There is also huge opposition, orchestrated by climate change campaigners, to the building of new coal-fired power stations, e.g. Kingsthorpe in Kent, as the carbon storage and capture technology that claims to make these power stations 'clean' is unlikely to be available mainstream for nearly 30 years. Currently there is a budget (as part of the push for green energy development) for four test bed sites in areas such as the Northumberland–Durham coast.

As nuclear power stations reach the end of their life, a major controversy which affects many coastal 'rural' areas is whether to build a new generation. Currently the government is looking at a period of planning and site approval, with the first build starting in 2013, and commissioning by 2017 (a date that many see as wildly optimistic). Nuclear power may make a comeback because renewables such as wind and solar energy are unlikely to bridge the 'energy gap' alone.

The building of nuclear power plants particularly affects the so called Energy Coast of west Cumbria (Figure 3.3), which the government sees as spearheading the development because of its experience in nuclear development and the world-renowned 'nuclear' skills of the local workforce.

Figure 3.3
Map of the Energy Coast

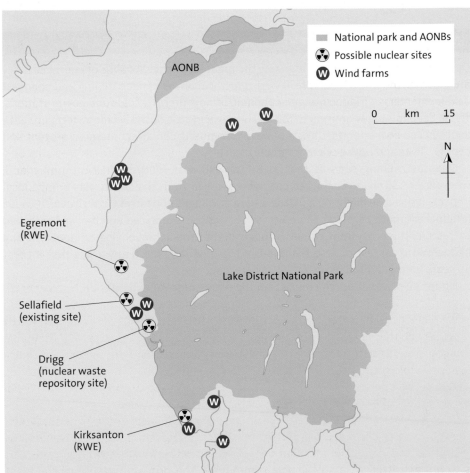

Contemporary Case Studies

The government criteria for new sites include being located near existing nuclear sites or close to where electricity is needed, or having suitable national grid connections. However, the three companies involved, RWE, EDF and E.ON, are looking beyond the existing sites at Sellafield, including the tiny hamlet of Kirksanton, well outside the current area, where there is huge opposition from local people as businesses such as bed and breakfast, caravan parks and farms will be threatened. Moreover, a very efficient windfarm may have to close.

While in west Cumbria there is general recognition that the nuclear industry is of enormous economic benefit to the area, as each facility provides over 600 jobs in an area with some of the highest unemployment in Britain, there are local concerns about issues of health (leukaemia clusters), threats of terrorism and toxic waste, especially as the area has the prospect of becoming home (at Drigg) to the UK's high-tech nuclear waste dump.

The prospect of a chain of new nuclear power stations along the coast has led protest groups to rename the area 'Lake District Nuclear Park', as it is only just outside the Lake District National Park, where planning permission for nuclear power stations and even windfarms would be automatically refused.

Small-scale energy developments

The notion that the world's peak in oil supply has passed and that rising demand will lead to a generally upward trend in prices has made small-scale land-based developments a more viable prospect. Currently there are 144 wells producing oil and gas (200 million barrels equivalent per year) and 157 licences for exploration, with 97 more likely to be issued, stretching from Dorset to Kent. They are in rolling downlands, often in beautiful countryside, and often in AONBs.

Many farmers and landowners see the land rent from oil and gas wells as the ultimate diversification, as it brings in £20 000–£50 000 per year. In general the 'nodding donkeys' are not especially conspicuous, as there are still stringent planning controls, but the 35-metre-high prospecting rigs can be very intrusive, with noise, visual and light pollution combined with the issue of the 64 lorries per day taking out overburden. This has caused huge conflicts in the beautiful, quiet village of Coldharbour in Surrey. The residents claim oil drilling will drive away the 600 000 visitors per year. In those rural downland villages there is very strong opposition from the wealthy middle classes, who perceive the prospect of even small-scale oil and gas development as completely damaging to the countryside and have organised themselves into powerful local pressure groups.

It might be expected that small-scale developments would be less likely to generate huge opposition. In fact, where the developments are generated by a bottom-up green movement, as is the case for the proposed Settle hydroelectric scheme in North Yorkshire, or the local energy revolution in the Peak District to create 'Sustainable Youlgrave' on the basis of hydro, solar photo-voltaics, mini-wind turbines and efficiency savings, whole communities can be mobilised in support. New government initiatives (2009) will encourage rural communities to develop renewable schemes and then make money by selling the electricity generated to the National Grid.

On the other hand, where a developer imposes a scheme such as the proposed (2008) biomass combined heat and power plant in Bishop's Castle, Shropshire, there is enormous opposition, in spite of the fact that one of the strategies of the town (see page 101) is to rebrand itself as a sustainable community. The primary purpose of the plant

transmit the power to the urban areas a high-voltage power line is needed (usually very ugly), with the direct route running straight through the newly designated Cairngorms National Park. The more aesthetically pleasing undersea/underground cables would be much more expensive. A super-grid system is clearly needed to overcome the variability of supply of renewables, by linking them to other sources, if they are to be more than a 'niche' provider.

(a) Anaerobic digestion

(b) Biofuels

(c) Nuclear

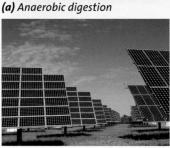
(d) Solar

(e) Tidal and wave

(f) Windpower

Fotolia

Figure 3.4 *Alternative sources of energy*

Questions

Study the photos of alternative energy options.
- (a) Suggest reasons why rural groups are often opposed to having alternative energy schemes such as the ones shown 'in their backyard'.
- (b) How might government policies impact on the development of rural areas for energy use?
- (c) Use a technique to evaluate the options shown.

Guidance

- (a) Imposition by central government on local areas. National energy shortages at the expense of local conservation. Likely to have a high environmental impact (use matrices to show this) with comparatively little economic benefit (nuclear does provide jobs). Failure to consult local people — planning enquiries seen as something to oppose.
- (b) On one hand freeing up planning legislation to push through developments could proliferate schemes. On the other hand new grants for community schemes (as used regularly in Germany) and the chance of selling back energy at a profit to the National Grid may damp down nimbyism and secure local approval and cooperation, i.e. local people become stakeholders.
- (c) Devise your own environmental and economic cost–benefit matrix.

Water

It is inevitable that more demands will be made on the countryside for water storage and use. This results from increasing demands for water from a rising population (more usage in agriculture for irrigation and in industry for processing in many parts of the world) combined with more uncertainty of supplies as a result of overabstraction and the impact of climate change, There are conflicts about the development of new supplies by creating reservoirs (*Case study 15*) or modifying surface water supplies such as rivers by damming or diversions, which have a very bad environmental impact on river and wetland ecosystems. *Case study 16* explores a recent mega-dam controversy. Conflicts occur with water transfers, as invariably water is diverted from rural areas to satisfy the demands of urban dwellers, or water is drawn from upstream of a catchment, which has an impact on downstream supplies.

Conflicts can escalate to wars if the supply is transnational, i.e. an aquifer or a river is shared by several countries. There is also a problem when several users are competing for diminishing supplies from the same river (*Case study 17*).

A NEW RESERVOIR FOR SOUTHEAST ENGLAND

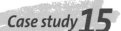

Case study *15*

The onset of climate change and more frequent summer droughts combined with escalating demand from a growing population means future demands will exceed supply in the Thames region.

A number of options have been considered, and those passing tests for acceptable economic and environmental costs include reservoir storage in southwest Oxfordshire, near Abingdon, which would capture water from the Thames during high flows and supply the upper Thames area and the Thames during low flow. The reservoir would be half the size of Lake Windermere and would be the largest stretch of open water in southern England. It is a major project, as rather than dig a hole the contractors would construct a 9 km-long embankment up to 25 m high to store the water. There has been lots of opposition; concern about the pollution levels and noise of lorries during construction, the problems of maintaining the quality of the water in terms of oxygen, algal and temperature characteristics, and also about loss of high-grade agricultural land and the visual impact of the new embankment feature. The £1 billion cost will fall on Thames Water customers — not only for the reservoir but also for the two-way pipeline to the Thames. Other residents are concerned about increased traffic flows if the proposed boat park and water sports area are developed. Alternatives to the reservoir include water transfers from Wales or a desalination plant in the Thames estuary.

Dams and their consequences

Dams not only provide water for irrigated food production (40% of all irrigated land) but are also usually multi-purpose. To justify the investment made, they are used to generate HEP, to enable flood control and to provide reservoirs for domestic use, and for development of tourism. But at what cost? Globally an estimated 85 million people have lost their homes and livelihoods and have been forced to move because of dam and reservoir construction. Dam construction and diversion channels play havoc with existing river levels and ecosystems, destroying fisheries and damaging wetlands and wildlife (the Yangtze river dolphin is now considered extinct).

Between 1930 and 1950, dams were seen as environmentally sound, as they produced large quantities of clean energy (HEP) and improved many aspects of the economy, such as food security. However, since the 1970s, as dams have increased in size and many of the best natural sites have been used, environmental concerns and human rights issues have combined to restrict dam construction, as it has so many negative impacts on the surrounding rural (often pristine wilderness) areas. The World Commission on Dams questioned the validity of many mega-dams, such as the Three Gorges Dam (China has over 40% of the world's 45 000 dams), arguing that the environmental costs outweigh the economic benefits. The case study of the Omo dams (*Case study 16*) shows how controversial dams can be — the opposition actually tried to get the building of Gibe III stopped 2 years after it began.

Case study **16** — OMO DAMS

Figure 3.5 shows the position of the Gibe III dam (currently Africa's second biggest). Gibe III, which is under construction, is the third in a series of HEP projects on the River Omo, which flows southwestwards out of Ethiopia towards Lake Turkana in Kenya.

Ethiopia is a very poor country — not only will 1800 megawatts of electricity be vital for Ethiopia's development but the surplus will be sold to neighbouring countries, including Djibouti, Yemen, Kenya, Uganda, Sudan and Egypt, earning $410 million in foreign exchange per year, and helping neighbours develop.

While an environmental assessment by the African Development Bank for private investors who funded the dam stated that Gibe III posed no major environmental threats, many groups have very different views.

International Rivers (a US NGO), Friends of Lake Turkana and a pressure group led by the well-known anthropologist Richard Leakey, formerly head of the Kenya Wildlife Service, all hold the view that the dam will cause an environmental disaster, not only because it could lower levels on Lake Turkana, already threatened by climate change, and so threaten ecosystems, but also for the indigenous peoples whose livelihoods depend on the lake, most of whom live in neighbouring Kenya.

The Ethiopian government also cited flood control as a bonus of the scheme, as it will regulate the flow of the River Omo. However, many of the 500 000 tribal subsistence farmers living by the lower Omo rely on the flood waters for their cultivation, as they follow a seasonal nomadic pattern based on water supply. As the river's waters retreat, tribes such as the Mursi colonise the floodplain in order to grow cereal crops. Tribal lands are already under threat from the newly developed national parks and from expropriation by large commercial farms that have capitalised on the irrigated water now available from earlier Omo dams. As many tribesmen habitually carry Kalashnikov or M16 assault rifles (Figure 3.6), disputes over grazing or water rights frequently escalate into bloody warfare. As with many controversies, the issues are very complex.

Figures 3.5 *The Omo River and Gibe dams*

Figure 3.6 *Armed Mursi tribesman*

John Warburton-Lee Photography/Alamy

The third type of water conflict involves competition for increasingly scarce resources, often between traditional subsistence farmers and new developers.

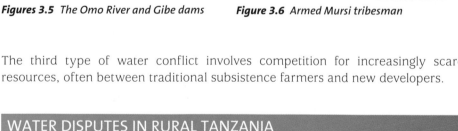

WATER DISPUTES IN RURAL TANZANIA

Case study 17

Figure 3.7 locates the Great Ruaha Catchment, from which water flows into the Usangu basin. The issue is that since the mid-1990s the Great Ruaha, always with a variable regime, has ceased flowing in the dry season, possibly because the water levels in the Ihefu wetlands have dropped below those required to feed the river. This low flow is a critical problem for the activities of a number of users, such as the generation of HEP, the maintenance of a wetland site for the wildlife and visitors to Ruaha National Park, and also rice farming. It has also led to conflict between the various users as supplies have dwindled. Users are shown in Figure 3.7.

Table 3.3 summarises the various viewpoints regarding how and why the wetlands, the reservoirs and the river were drying up. Originally it was thought that the drying-up of the wetland, rivers and reservoirs was connected, as a result of overgrazing, impacts of climate change and deforestation.

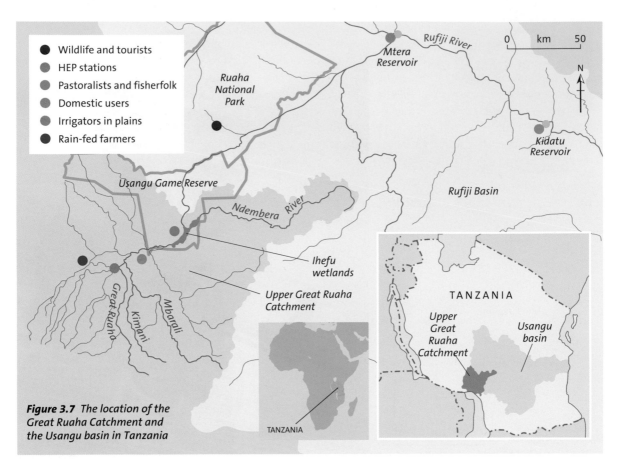

Figure 3.7 *The location of the Great Ruaha Catchment and the Usangu basin in Tanzania*

Table 3.3 *Viewpoints on hydrological changes in the Usangu basin and Ruaha Catchment*

Stakeholder group	Initial viewpoint regarding causes, 1995	Main viewpoint, 2004, after scientific study
General view	Shrinking wetland may cause low reservoir levels and low flow in rivers	Identifies three separate issues
Scientific investigation	Tested cattle overgrazing, deforestation, climate change, irrigation abstraction, flows into reservoirs	Found overabstraction in dry season main cause; also miscalculation of draw-down of stored water from reservoir
Friends of Ruaha and WWF	Overuse of water in dry season for large-scale irrigation; damaged wetlands from overgrazing	Overabstraction in dry season damaged wetlands
Ministry of Agriculture	Inefficient smallholder schemes take much of the water, starving those downstream	Smallholders compete over water, so their management is increasingly efficient
Ministry of Natural Resources	Cattle and overgrazing are degrading wetland; deforestation in upper catchment is reducing base flow	Cattle, overgrazing and deforestation remain problems
Ministry of Water	Inefficient smallholder schemes; deforestation of upper catchment	Inefficient smallholder schemes
Mbarali District	Cattle and overgrazing in wetland and deforestation in the upper catchment are leading to water shortages	These problems remain
Electricity Supply Company	Scale and inefficiency of irrigation lead to lack of water for power generation	Scale and inefficiency of irrigation lead to lack of water for power generation (i.e. no change in view)

A research programme suggested that mismanagement of water release from the reservoirs, and increasing abstraction for domestic use and irrigation of the rice in the dry seasons, were the main problems. Table 3.3 shows how in spite of the scientific survey most stakeholders persisted in their views as to assignation of guilt: essentially downstream stakeholders blamed poor farmers upstream for overuse.

The way ahead is Integrated Water Resources Management (IWRM), which brings all stakeholders together to decide how to meet long-term needs for water while maintaining essential ecological services and economic benefits, by considering the interconnected nature of hydrological resources.

In conclusion, there are many other conflicts about using the rural landscape for development of resources. Essentially the conflicts are of two major types:

- Conflicts over the actual exploitation of the resource, with large-scale operations creating the greatest impact. Top-down developments by TNCs or similar bodies in response to government policies are far more at risk from opposition than bottom-up, more sustainable schemes.
- Conflicts between stakeholders, who have different visions for the countryside and require the resource for different proposals that may conflict with each other (a common feature in the case of lakes and reservoirs).

Using case studies 8

(a) Search on the internet for 'superquarries in Scotland' and draw a conflict matrix to show the views for and against their development (e.g. Lingen, Harris).

(b) Rank the following six developments in terms of their likely ability to attract opposition from local rural people. Justify your rank order.
incinerator; superquarry; Centre Parcs-style holiday village; large-scale opencast development for iron or coal; large-scale windfarm; mega-dam

Guidance

(a) Superquarries are a major issue because of their size, the visually huge scar they cause on the side of a hill, issues of dust and noise, and also the movement of lorries removing overburden and transporting the rock to ports for export. They are very capital-intensive, but could provide key jobs in areas with high unemployment (c. 15%). The location is especially controversial — Harris, for example, is an area of outstanding natural beauty. For additional information, see *Case study 18*.

(b) Develop criteria for assessment:
  - environmental impact — dust, noise, smell, visual impact, possible air/water pollution, lorries/transport
  - economic benefit — value of investment, multiplier effect, local jobs, local benefits

  Then use a scoring system to rank the six developments and justify your choice.

Conflicts in remote rural areas

Remote rural areas are characterised by their harsh physical environments, sparse population densities and long distances from high-level services. Remote areas are frequently fragile environments, highly vulnerable to tourists seeking a 'wilderness'

Conservation needs
Most remote rural areas have landscapes and ecosystems of high geodiversity and biodiversity, which are both fragile and vulnerable. Many areas are therefore designated as some type of protected or conservation area such as a national park.

PRESSURES ON REMOTE AREAS

Community needs
All upland areas contain settlements; providing for community needs for a basic quality of life is a major issue. Farmers and estate owners manage the land; other land users, such as quarry owners, forestry, water board, military training, provide jobs for the community, but can cause damage to the landscape. Many communities are very fragile and are undergoing change as a result of migration.

Recreation needs
All remote upland areas are popular for a range of outdoor activities, from walking and mountain biking to kayaking, all with varying impacts on the environment (especially as there is now 'a right to roam'). **Honeypot** areas are a particular issue; facilities are needed for these visitors. Moreover, employment and tourism are a key source of income for many in the community.

Figure 3.8
The conflict of needs in remote rural areas

experience. They are also frequently areas of deprivation and **social exclusion**. As Figure 3.8 shows, there is a need to balance the conflicting interests of three major groups.

Remote rural areas vary tremendously according to the nature of the scenery, the ownership of the land, the range and scale of pressures, the profile of the communities that live there and the degree of management. The next case study looks at the Isle of Harris in the Outer Hebrides, one of the remotest areas in the UK.

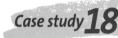

Case study **18** ECONOMIC LIFELINE OR BUREAUCRATIC STRAITJACKET?

On 20 February 2009 a vote took place in which 71.6% of the residents of the Isle of Harris took part. Seven hundred and thirty-two said yes to the proposal that Harris become Scotland's third national park — a move designed to save the island — but 311 were against, showing how controversial the proposal is.

Arguments for

1 Many people who voted for the proposal felt that national park status would reverse the chronic population decline and create jobs by boosting tourism. Between 1981 and 2001 the population in Harris fell by 24%. Primary school rolls fell from 179 to 131 and secondary school rolls fell from 141 to 109, resulting in school closures. Currently nearly 14% of the population are over 65 — a demographic time bomb, as there are high levels of out-migration, especially of 18–30-year-olds, and a very low birth rate, leading to marked depopulation. There are now only 2000 people living on the island, and by 2030 this total may halve. A declining population poses serious problems for the provision of viable services.

2 Tourism is growing only at a slow rate. Harris is a hidden gem, with only 117 000 visitors per year. It is argued that achieving national park status would generate more tourism (a possible increase of 20–50%). The new status would provide 20 jobs directly for trained professionals. Indirectly, national park status should give a boost to

Western Isles businesses that benefit from tourism (Harris Tweed, restaurants, hotels etc.), perhaps creating a further 160 jobs. It would also lead to diversification of the crofts and add value to farm produce through national park branding. Currently unemployment is as high as 20% (excluding part-time crofting for subsistence).

3 The idea is very much a bottom-up initiative from the Harris people themselves, who saw the need for **rebranding** of the island to safeguard its future. They argue that national park status would not threaten the unique physical and cultural environment but enhance it. The North Harris Community Trust has already bought the North Harris and Loch Seaforth estates, and a possible purchase of the West Harris estate could lead to the local community owning 60% of the island. The national park would extend the concept of community involvement, although the park would function under Scottish national park regulations, with a park board on which Harris people would serve.

Arguments against

1 Park planning boards have traditionally had very strict planning rules. Some islanders argue that national park status would be bad for the fragile economy, as large-scale developments would be prohibited on environmental grounds. An example of such a development is Lingen Bay, where the plans for a new superquarry were finally rejected on environmental grounds, although the development could have created 40 skilled jobs. More red tape than ever is the concern.

Joe Gough/Fotolia

Figure 3.9
Isle of Harris

2 House prices have tended to rise on the designation of national park status, as the profile of the area is raised. In a low-wage economy, affordable housing is vital to stem out-migration. The desire for second homes and retirement cottages pushes up prices, and Harris will be seen as ultra-desirable in this respect.

3 National park status could create further pressures on the environment as more visitors arrive. This could threaten the mountainous physical landscape, the unpolluted beaches and the rare wildlife (otters, eagles, seals etc.), as well as diluting the unique Gaelic culture based on the Gaelic language.

9 Questions

Using case studies

(a) **What exactly is so special about the environment and culture of Harris? (Research pictures online of mountains, beaches, archaeological sites etc.)**

(b) **What evidence is there of rural deprivation on Harris? (Investigate ageing population in decline, out-migration, high rates of unemployment, closure of services.)**

(c) **Evaluate the evidence for and against the plan — will it be an economic lifeline or a bureaucratic straitjacket? (Use two columns to summarise the arguments.)**

Many remote rural areas include areas of outstanding natural beauty, or of unique geodiversity or biodiversity. The most common large-scale designation is national park status. Globally there are nearly 7000 national parks, covering some 60% of the total 20 million hectares of protected areas. The conservation status of national parks varies from country to country, but essentially all aim to conserve landscape of outstanding quality while allowing the public varying degrees of access to enjoy the scenery for recreation. In some national parks, such as those in the USA, all the land is owned by the government. In the UK the land is owned by a patchwork of agencies and individuals, and the government only exercises control through agencies such as the Forestry Commission and the Ministry of Defence (MOD). Conflicts are inevitable unless effective management strategies are developed by the park management authorities.

Case study 19 — CONFLICTS IN THE CAIRNGORMS NATIONAL PARK

The Cairngorms National Park (CNP) covers about 5% of Scotland's land area and is a near-pristine wilderness area. It has long been recognised as the most important area in Britain for nature conservation values. Within the park (Figure 3.10) nearly 40% of the land is designated as important for nature conservation and enjoys various levels of protection (SSSI, Ramsar conservation site — wetlands, National Nature Reserve and Natura 2000 site). The park itself is 75% privately owned, largely by great estates which provide sporting activities such as deer and grouse shooting. Sixteen thousand people live within the park, largely in small towns such as Braemar. The population has an

Figure 3.10
Issues to manage in Cairngorms National Park

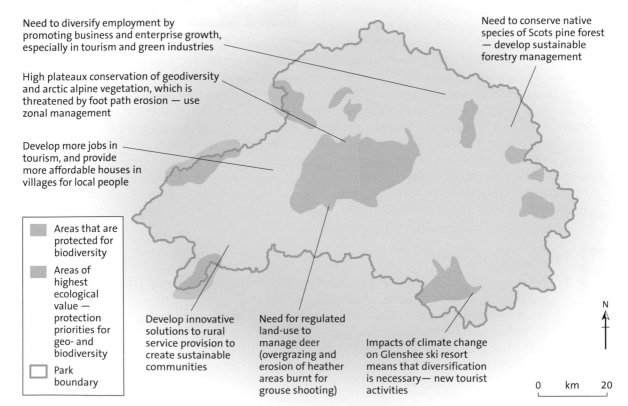

Need to diversify employment by promoting business and enterprise growth, especially in tourism and green industries

Need to conserve native species of Scots pine forest — develop sustainable forestry management

High plateaux conservation of geodiversity and arctic alpine vegetation, which is threatened by foot path erosion — use zonal management

Develop more jobs in tourism, and provide more affordable houses in villages for local people

Areas that are protected for biodiversity

Areas of highest ecological value — protection priorities for geo- and biodiversity

Park boundary

Develop innovative solutions to rural service provision to create sustainable communities

Need for regulated land-use to manage deer (overgrazing and erosion of heather areas burnt for grouse shooting)

Impacts of climate change on Glenshee ski resort means that diversification is necessary— new tourist activities

0   km   20

N

ageing structure due to in-migration of retired people and out-migration of the 18–30 age group as a result of a lack of affordable housing and well-paid jobs. Each year nearly 1.5 million people visit the park for a range of outdoor activities, including mountain biking, mountain walking and skiing. The future of the Cairngorms as Scotland's leading skiing centre is under threat from climate change, as snowfall is becoming more unpredictable.

Inevitably conflicts could occur between meeting the needs of the visitors, the needs of local people and the need to conserve the natural environment. The range of issues to manage is shown in Figure 3.10. The Cairngorms National Park 2007–12 Plan includes three priorities for action:

- conserving and enhancing the park's natural environment
- meeting the needs of those living and working in the park
- helping visitors to enjoy and understand the park

While many of these issues are prevalent in most remote rural upland areas, there are some which particularly apply to the Cairngorms (such as the skiing crisis and the deer problem). Issues within national parks are usually managed more actively than those outside.

10

Using case studies

(a) **Carry out further research at www.cairngorms.co.uk to make a detailed list of key issues. Using a two-column format, list the issues in one column and possible management solutions in the other.**

(b) **Research a contrasting national park, e.g. Yellowstone in the USA or a national park in east Africa (Masai Mara, Udzungwa etc.), and compare and contrast the key issues there.**

Guidance

Park in the USA — state-owned. Note in some cases Native Americans were cleared out, and conflicts about how to conserve have re-emerged as these people seek to reassert their rights.

East African park — research the degree to which sustainable development or use of extractive reserves is being used to assist the native people so that there will be support for conservation of wildlife (big game etc.) and other restrictions on activity in the park.

A further major conflict in remote rural areas concerns the provision of housing. It is a particular problem in areas such as the Yorkshire Dales, the Lake District National Park and coastal Cornwall, where a very restricted supply and huge demand has led to escalating prices, well beyond the means of local people. The ratio of average house prices to average wages is extremely unfavourable (see Figure 3.11). As people seek the rural idyll, often in remote upland areas (possibilities of teleworking or retirement havens), this puts even more pressure on the supply of housing. It is tempting to suggest that the desire for second and holiday homes is fuelling the rural housing crisis, but the reality is far more complex, as *Case study 20* shows.

The Affordable Rural Housing Commission recommended in 2005 that 11 000 affordable houses should be built each year in rural settlements in order to fulfil the need for subsidised homes that traditional rural dwellers can rent or purchase. It said that construction should use pockets of brownfield land available in many villages, e.g. disused industrial sites or garages.

Second homes are privately owned dwellings either used as family holiday homes or bought as an investment for commercial letting. They range from small summerhouses and holiday chalets to traditional cottages and large detached residences. While the chalets do not contribute to the housing problem, in general ordinary dwellings do, especially if they are not located in dedicated resort complexes.

Second homes are a feature of most developed countries. In Finland, for example, 17% of people own a second home and 50% have access to using one, but they are largely of the summerhouse type in an underpopulated country. In Sweden there are 700 000 second homes, and here there are more concerns because of their concentration around the lakes in central Sweden, a relatively crowded area.

A survey in the USA in 2009 revealed that there were 8.1 million vacation holiday homes (of which nearly 5 million had been purchased since 2003) and 40.5 million investment units. The median age of the owners was 46 years, and their annual income $100 000; 74% of owners were married, with 55% having no children under 18 at home. The average purchase price was $200 000 in 2007 and the average distance from home was 316 miles. The preferred location was in the south, especially Florida (45%), either in small towns and rural areas (49%) or in resorts (23%).

Governments aim to assist in the development of thriving and sustainable rural areas with strong rural economies. A sufficient supply of affordable housing is vital to achieve this. Many rural dwellers perceive that second homes are the root cause of a shortage of affordable appropriate housing in the countryside and the subsequent rural housing problems.

The main issues associated with them in the UK are as follows:

- Their purchase disadvantages first-time local, often low-income buyers if there is an open market, thus encouraging out-migration, as on average second home purchasers target the smaller, cheaper end, e.g. quaint cottages.
- They are perceived to represent conspicuous consumption and place a blight on village communities, as the second-homers only 'live' in the village for about 10% of the year and contribute little to village life or the support of village services — 'ghost villages' such as Chapel Stile in Cumbria where 40% of houses are second homes are an issue.
- The purchase of village housing that is already in short supply because of planning restrictions aimed at preventing village sprawl leads to escalation in house prices, which is a great problem in traditional rural areas with very low-wage economies. As house prices rise, even middle-income public sector workers are priced out of the market.
- In rural Wales there are additional cultural issues, as the English influx threatens the survival of Welsh communities by destroying their traditions, culture and language.

As Figure 3.11 shows, the key issue is the ratio of house prices to median incomes. In some areas house prices are between seven and 16 times more — i.e. unaffordable.

The evidence from a range of research would suggest, however, that second homes are not the root cause of rural housing problems:

- Second home ownership is actually either declining or static in most parts of the UK. Ownership peaked with an investment boom in the 1980s fuelled by double tax relief on mortgages. While a second peak did occur in the 1990s, investment abroad,

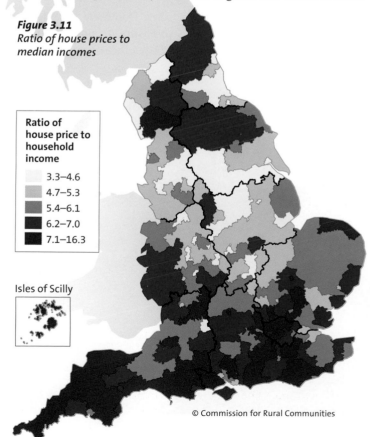

initially in France and Spain but more latterly in eastern Europe, is now seen as more lucrative. By 2006, legislation was in place for local authorities to charge the full amount of council tax on second homes.

■ By European standards, second home ownership in the UK is low — at under 5% in absolute terms when compared with Scandinavia (20%) or Spain (15%). However, England and Wales are two of the countries with the highest density of population and greatest housing supply shortage in Europe.

■ The lack of rural housing can be related to the restrictions in supply caused by planning laws in rural areas, which limit new buildings in many villages. Equally the 'right to buy' legislation led to a loss of social housing stock, which has not been replaced by housing association stock, thus leading to a lack of affordable housing.

■ There has been a rising desire to live in the country, with the population in many rural areas increasing steadily. The main pressures have come from people retiring to remote areas, commuters in accessible areas such as the Cotswolds, and to a more limited extent teleworkers, all much more numerically significant than second home dwellers, who overall only occupy around 150 000 homes.

The main issue concerning second homes, therefore, is not their number but their concentration. Inevitably second homes are located in key holiday areas such as national parks and coasts, i.e. they are not an endemic but an epidemic issue.

Table 3.4 shows the distribution of second home ownership in southwest England compared with England and Wales in 2007.

Figure 3.11
Ratio of house prices to median incomes

Ratio of house price to household income

- 3.3–4.6
- 4.7–5.3
- 5.4–6.1
- 6.2–7.0
- 7.1–16.3

Isles of Scilly

© Commission for Rural Communities

Table 3.4
The distribution of second home ownership in southwest England compared with England and Wales in 2007

Area	Second homes	Percentage of total
England and Wales	150 718	0.6
Cornwall and Scilly	10 787	4.6
Devon	11 108	3.5
Plymouth	336	0.3
Torbay	1234	2.0
Dorset	4939	2.8
Somerset	2023	0.9
CORNWALL		
Caradon	1385	3.8
Carrick	1462	3.5
Kerrier	1145	2.7
North Cornwall	3152	8.1
Penwith	2209	7.1
Restormel	1136	2.6
Isles of Scilly	298	24.8
DEVON		
East Devon	2170	3.5
Exeter	185	0.4
Mid Devon	345	1.1
North Devon	1774	4.4
South Hams	4492	11.1
Teignbridge	873	1.6
Torridge	892	3.3
West Devon	376	1.8

In the Isles of Scilly (25%) and within villages such as Port Isaac in north Cornwall (40%) or Portlemouth in South Hams, Devon (54%), there is clearly a localised crisis. In Wales, hotspots are found in coastal fringes such as Pembrokeshire National Park, the Lleyn Peninsula, Snowdonia or Anglesey. In Abersoch, in Lleyn, up to 40% of all homes are holiday homes and in Cwm-yr-Eglwys, a coastal hamlet near Newport, Dyfed, the critical threshold of second homes has been passed, with only 15% of houses occupied all year round. Even in the thriving settlement of Newport the issue is whether the short-lived summer tourist trade can create a concentrated multiplier effect sufficient to support the local shops.

For this reason, measures are being discussed in a number of these 'epidemic' areas which involve one of two strategies, essentially solving the supply side and controlling the demand side by housing market management. The provision of more affordable housing has certainly eased the problem of second home house price inflation in many parts of Wales, but in the Yorkshire Dales National Park the head of planning has explained that such is the great demand for housing in the Dales villages from outsiders that it would not be possible to build enough houses to bring prices down to levels affordable to local people. The Yorkshire Dales National Park has therefore worked with the North York Moors National Park and the Lake District National Park to develop a policy whereby new housing will be limited to needy locals and incomers taking up existing jobs within the area, with no permissions for conversions. Properties affected are expected to sell for a third less than the market price, with restrictive covenants in perpetuity — a similar system to that operated in Guernsey. This would resolve issues in villages such as Clapham and Austwick.

Other schemes include rural housing enablers, such as a HomeBuy scheme for young key workers and an empty homes usage strategy to ensure maximum letting. Scheme 151 can also be used to control the right to buy and therefore prevent the sale of local authority houses at inflated prices.

Figure 3.12
Clapham in the Yorkshire Dales National Park

David Hughes/Fotolia

Contemporary Case Studies

At the national level, the Affordable Rural Housing Commission aims to persuade county councils to set higher quotas of affordable houses for all development granted planning permission. Specific holiday villages and retirement villages are also being built, which again will not conflict with the local market.

When people consider remote upland regions they think above all of conflicts brought about by the advent of both day visitors and longer-stay tourists. There are numerous tales of trampling and footpath erosion, littering, pollution and congestion — in honeypot sites such as the Peak District or Lake District villages, or at World Heritage sites such as Machu Picchu, Peru. Conversely, for local people the jobs provided by tourism, albeit frequently low-paid and seasonal, are an absolute lifeline. They typify the conflict between meeting the needs of tourists and local people, and the need to conserve the environment and heritage of these remote rural areas.

The rural–urban fringe: a zone of rapid change and potential conflicts

The rural–urban fringe, which can be described as 'the countryside around towns' is the meeting point of both rural and urban influences. It is therefore a highly contested environment, containing a diverse array of activities — part-rural, part-urban — which frequently do not mix. As it is a zone of rapid change, pressures for its development can lead to conflicts about competing demands.

Figure 3.13 summarises the socio-cultural and economic reasons for the pressures.

The main conflicts are between developers and conservationists, between urban expansionists and traditional rural people (for example, problems for farmers from dogs, vandalism and fly-tipping) and between newcomers and original inhabitants.

Socio-cultural changes
- **Demand for more recreation space:** golf courses, sports facilities
- **Increased car ownership:** road building, commuter settlements
- **Increased affluence:** retail parks, money to spend on recreation
- **Increased affluence:** larger, better housing; airport expansion
- **Increased number of households:** housing demand
- **Fear of crime, pollution:** counterurbanisation; infill in villages
- **Environmental awareness:** more conservation areas
- **Teleworking:** housing demand outside urban area

→ Demand for rural–urban fringe land ←

Economic changes
- **Shift from rail-freight to road-freight:** road building
- **Increasingly footloose industry:** large, greenfield sites on trunk roads
- **Increasing industrial competition:** sites with good access
- **High urban land prices:** lower cost urban edge sites
- **Lack of inner-city space:** city-edge sites
- **Universal car ownership:** commuting

Figure 3.13
Pressures on the rural–urban fringe

The rural–urban fringe round any large city consists of an area extending between 10 km and 50 km outward from the edge of the city. In developed countries planning regulations are heavily used to control the pace and nature of development, so in effect the rural–urban fringe usually consists of two zones: the **green belt,** which is largely farmland, and the commuter belt beyond (Figure 3.14). In the UK 20% of all land can be classified as rural–urban fringe land.

Figure 3.14
The rural–urban fringe in a developed country

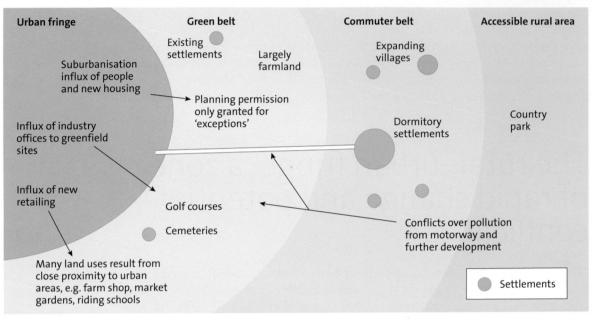

Factors determining the character of a particular rural–urban fringe and the precise nature of the conflicts include the following:

- The level of development that influences what stage of the urbanisation cycle a country has reached. In developing countries the main process is rural-to-urban, i.e. centripetal, migration, which puts pressure on the land for construction of shanty towns for new arrivals. In developed countries the main process is counterurbanisation, i.e. a centrifugal movement that can lead to urban sprawl unless controlled by planning.
- The nature of the migrants. In developing countries they are frequently young, often male, and relatively poor, so the urban periphery can become a 'septic fringe' with local forests degraded for fuelwood and widespread environmental pollution from sewage, waste and thousands of cooking stoves. In contrast, in developed countries most migrants are richer people who migrate out of the city for a perceived better quality of life (filtering). Sometimes they take up 'hobby' farming or 'horsiculture' and commute to work. Congestion on inadequate roads is a major issue.
- The orientation, accessibility and affordability of transport links into the city. Better networks lead to more rapid development.
- The physical terrain and environmental barriers beyond the existing built-up area. These play a major part in influencing the type of land use and the shape of any development.

Contemporary Case Studies

- The land values, existing land use types and land-terrain systems around the expanding city. These may determine the precise balance of the 'good' and the 'ugly' (see Table 3.5), and also in emerging economic powers such as India and China there are huge conflicts between farmers and the developers who need the land for new factories and businesses (*Case study 22*).

- The precise designation of the administrative and political boundaries and the extent to which they coincide with the de facto urban boundaries. The boundaries may or may not allow the town to grow into the rural–urban fringe or they may separate the urban area from its natural rural hinterland and lead to conflict.

- Most importantly, the degree of existing planning legislation. This can control development (as is the case with green belt legislation); alternatively a lack of it can facilitate development.

- The political system. Note how in Communist countries all rural land is owned directly or indirectly by the government, so can be 'taken over' (land grabbed).

In conclusion, there are many characteristics that are common to all rural–urban fringe zones — diversity of land use, rapid change and the juxtaposition of the good, the bad, and the downright ugly!

Table 3.5 summarises the range

Land use	The 'good'	The 'ugly'
Agricultural	Many well-managed and manicured market gardens and smallholdings Lots of 'horsiculture' Abundant farm shops and pick-your-own businesses	Fragmented farms, struggling for survival, frequently suffering from litter, trespass and vandalism; some left derelict in expectation of planning permission being granted and a huge profit made
Development	Some well-sited, well-landscaped developments in the form of new enterprise and science parks, although there is often talk about how planning permission was obtained if in a green belt	Some developments such as out-of-town retail parks can bring heavy pollution and traffic congestion; many small-scale, semi-illicit businesses, e.g. caravan storage and junk yards, can arise
Urban services	Some, e.g. reservoirs, can be reasonably attractive	Others, such as mineral works, sewage works, landfill sites or even Sunday markets can be eyesores
Transport and infrastructure	Some new green ways and cycle ways to give countryside access	Motorways carve up countryside and promote even more development Airport development is a major cause for conflict
Recreation and sport	Country parks and golf courses can lead to conservation; sports fields provide attractive open spaces and provide vital leisure facilities	Some areas can be run down or used for noisy events, e.g. stock car racing, scrambling or even 'raves'
Landscape and nature conservation	Some high-quality countryside, many SSSIs and AONBs; some 'edge lands' have huge eco-potential as they have been allowed to become wild	Much degraded or deteriorated land, e.g. that ruined by fly-tipping (67% of all farmland); many SSSIs under threat from development

Table 3.5
Land use: the 'good' and the 'ugly'

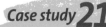

Newcastle City Council developed the concept of a sustainable urban extension in order to develop its very accessible northern fringe area.

While this extension is on previously green belt land and is therefore highly controversial, it has to be set in context.

- It is a vital part of Newcastle's 'Going for Growth' strategy. Regeneration and restructuring of Newcastle's inner city areas are proceeding apace, but the city population (especially affluent middle classes) is declining because of a lack of housing choice, so an urban extension was deemed necessary.
- There was already huge pressure on the green belt area for new leisure development (horse racing and premier division rugby) as well as more retail parks, and the expansion of Newcastle International Airport.
- There was also a great need to attract high-profile high-tech companies to provide more jobs for professional and managerial workers. These companies demand attractive greenfield sites.

Figure 3.15
Newcastle Great Park — a new housing development on the edge of Newcastle upon Tyne

- The green belt strategy in other parts of Newcastle was tightened so that green corridors and green wedges could be guaranteed for the whole of the city.

Newcastle Great Park (Figure 3.15) has caused tremendous conflicts between the developers and conservationists. Perceived economic gains (possibly up to 8000 new jobs over 10 years, 2500 new homes and many other new facilities) were outweighed

Housing is built at a high density; many homes are three-storey townhouses

The development is located on the northern edge of Newcastle, on former greenbelt land

House prices are in the range £250 000–£800 000

About 20% of land is landscaped open space and woodland

This reed pond filters urban runoff from houses and roads

Cycle paths and a regular bus service are provided

Employment is close by in a new business park — this is the HQ of Sage, a software company

All photographs supplied by Cameron Dunn

for some by the environmental loss of over 500 hectares of good-quality, high-amenity agricultural land.

The plan was also sold on the basis that it would be a green, sustainable urban extension, in the following ways:

- Under a 'two for one' scheme the builders pledged to build two homes on brownfield land for every one built on green belt or greenfield land.
- Half of all the land would be parkland or open land, giving opportunities for wildlife conservation.
- Above all, sustainable transport strategies were developed with a reliance on good-quality public transport with 40 km of paths and cycle-ways. Local services would be provided to develop self-sustaining communities not reliant on car use. Park and ride would be developed.
- Sustainable energy and waste technology was used, with many homes built with solar panels etc.

11 Questions

Using case studies

(a) Prepare a justification for the development of Newcastle's northern green belt.

(b) To what extent do you consider the development of Newcastle's northern green belt to be genuinely sustainable?

Guidance

(a) Provide details of the need for high-value housing for professionals and high-quality 'pro jobs' in high-tech industry, neither of which favour city centre location — also the need for good access to motorway and airport.

(b) Define sustainability — builders' 'two for one' policy and the development of various sustainable features.

THE RURAL–URBAN FRINGE IN CHINA

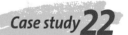
Case study **22**

In China all land is owned by the state, but only in urban areas is there direct ownership — in rural areas it is owned by the rural collectives, in effect Communist Party committees which lease the land to farmers for a period of 30 years in plots proportional to their family size. Once an area is declared urban — a frequent event in China, as rapid urbanisation is occurring (as in many NICs) and there is huge demand for new land for urban development on the edge of cities — the state can compulsorily take over villages and land for urban development.

In Chengdu, the capital of Sichuan, 12 urban villages are being built in southern Winhou. In each village, developers are building apartment blocks to house 50 000 people, new factories and new commercial and biome facilities. Urban districts need to make money from new developments, as they are recovering less money in grants from central government. Compulsory 'land grabs' from farmers in the rural–urban fringe are a major issue in China — in the last 5 years 50 000 land disputes have been recorded in 224 urban districts. While the farmers do not own the land, much of it is high-quality arable land, and the demolition of their houses and loss of livelihoods for development is devastating. They are given compensation and the option of a house in the new development (often 2–3 years later), but many argue that there is a need for reform in the land acquisition process.

Rapid urbanisation is also influencing the nature of farming in the rural–urban fringe. Many rural collectives have expanded into commercial enterprises such as large-scale fish farming, dairy and pig units and market gardening. In particular, as the Chinese have become more affluent, this has led to a diet revolution with the rising popularity of animal protein. This has again changed the landscape. In some areas land has been bought by pharmaceutical and agrochemical TNCs which are using it to experiment with highly intensive fertiliser-based farming, or with GM crops. While there are environmental implications to these developments in China, the acquisition of land for development is the main cause for conflict. While the rural committees eye the profits, it is the traditional farmers and their families who suffer.

Rural futures

There are a number of scenarios for the future of rural areas (Figure 4.1). A business as usual approach (1) can be adopted that promotes development at rates similar to those of today. CPRE developed a nightmare vision for the UK in 2035 resulting from this scenario, with 7 million more homes, nearly half the greenfield sites used up, highly specialised farms using GM crops, 40 million cars on the roads (many of them rural), a turnstile countryside with timed tickets granting access to top views, and an ever increasing range of 'commodified' activities causing a very artificial-looking rural environment.

A more sustainable approach could be adopted — this might emphasise environmental sustainability (2), whereby landscape conservation is the priority, or socio-cultural sustainability (3), where the cohesiveness of the rural communities and their quality of life are the main focus. In an ideal world, all-round sustainability (4) should be the target, whereby environmental conservation is balanced with ensuring a high quality of life for local people, who are fully involved in decision making.

These four scenarios, which are applicable in all rural areas (shown in Figure 4.1), were first developed by Natural England in the UK in 2006.

Figure 4.1
Four scenarios for the future of the countryside

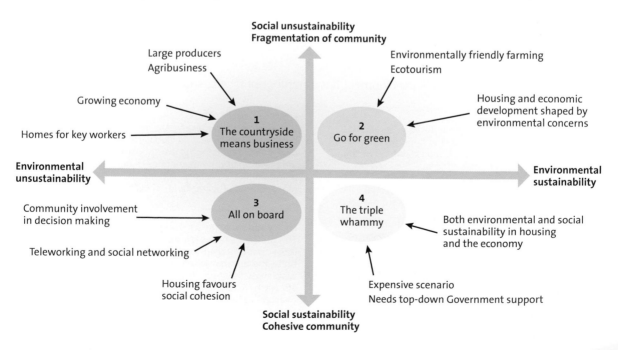

Rural Development & the Countryside

The results of the chosen scenarios will be to produce completely different 'brands' of countryside:

- A green countryside — an environmental paradise that will please environmental idealists and also farmers in their new role as environmental stewards but will be opposed by agribusiness, house builders, and developers in general.
- A consumer countryside — where income from consumption predominates over production and environmental concerns. This countryside would appeal to 'local foodies', tourists, and urbanites seeking a rural idyll.
- An inclusive countryside — accessible to the poor and ethnic minorities as well as middle classes and traditional rural dwellers. This may be difficult to manage as there will be conflicting views.
- A pragmatic countryside — one that works. Green, consumer or inclusive values will not be imposed on the countryside, but will be able to exist side by side and be welded into a functional mosaic of competing uses that provides a good quality of life for all country dwellers.

In an interconnected globalised world, there will inevitably be parallel influences on rural futures, notably the drive towards sustainability and the widespread exploitation of new information and communications technology. Nevertheless, developed and developing rural areas are very different in character and in the changes they are experiencing. There are therefore different solutions to provide secure rural futures.

The first set of case studies explores sustainable futures. The next group of case studies looks at how new technology is revolutionising the lives of the rural poor, especially in developing countries. The last batch explores rural 'rebranding', which some developed countries are exploring in order to find an improved economic future for rural areas.

Sustainable development of the countryside

Figure 4.2
The sustainability
quadrant

Sustainable development has a number of facets, shown in Figure 4.2.

Futurity
Present generations should leave future generations the ability to maintain present standards of living, whether through natural or cultural capital. So we are entitled to use up finite natural resources only if we provide future generations with the know-how (through improved science, technology and social organisation) to maintain living standards from what is left. This is the Brundtland principle.

Environment
We should seek to preserve the integrity of ecosystems, both at the local level and globally at the scale of the biosphere, in order not to disrupt natural processes that are essential to the safeguarding of human life and to maintaining biodiversity. This includes the eco-friendly management of water, land, wildlife, forests etc.

Public participation
The public should be aware of, and participate in, the process of change towards sustainable development in line with Rio Summit (1992) Principle 10. Environmental issues are best handled with the participation of all concerned citizens. Each individual should have the information and opportunity to participate in the decision-making process (bottom-up).

Equity and social justice
This principle implies fair shares for all including the most disadvantaged, locally and globally. 'If there is a finite amount that we may consume or use beyond which we cannot go... then we must share what we already have far more than is currently the case. Equality of access to the world's global resources therefore must be the guiding principle, improving the lives of the poor' (Johannesburg 2002).

In rural areas sustainable policies need to be designed to:

■ conserve the countryside and the natural resources for future generations (Brundtland principle of futurity); increasingly this can mean adopting climate-proofing strategies that allow communities to adapt to climate change

■ develop green strategies for the use of resources such as energy and water and for economic activities such as tourism (in particular **ecotourism** — see page 83)

■ develop equitable strategies that meet the economic and social needs of all rural dwellers, for example by improving the viability of services, and providing employment for all, in particular developing pro-poor strategies to bring the most disadvantaged rural dwellers out of poverty and exclusion — a particular issue in developing areas where rural poverty is epidemic

■ initiate strategies that involve local people in planning and providing for their futures via bottom-up development strategies. Community involvement is a key facet of socio-cultural stability. Often governments have to learn to consult local people and involve them: in the case of the Udzungwa national park in Tanzania, a top-down environmental conservation project, this meant involving them in strategies such as hunting and fuel-gathering bans within the park, and providing them with alternative means of existence in order to ensure success (see *Case study 25*).

It is worth remembering that, as the four scenarios would suggest, it is a fine balancing act to ensure environmental, economic and socio-cultural sustainability. This is demonstrated by the following case study on eco-towns.

ECO-TOWNS IN THE UK
Case study **23**

The government definition of eco-town highlights the tensional forces: eco-towns are a combined response to the challenges of climate change, the need for more sustainable living, and the need to increase housing supply, especially of affordable housing. Eco-towns are designed to be 'small new towns of between 5000 and 20 000 houses, for the twenty-first century, with sustainability standards significantly above equivalent levels in existing towns'. These eco-towns will act as test beds for all manner of sustainable technology. They will not be entirely self-sufficient, so must be linked to existing major settlements by high-quality public transport.

The problem is the precise locations of these towns, all in rural areas — from a shortlist of 15, the final choice of sites has been narrowed down to four sites for the first wave (Figure 4.3):

1 Whitehill Bordon, Hampshire, built on a former MoD site — minimal local opposition.

2 Imerys China Clay Community near St Austell, Cornwall — needed to regenerate an area in great decline.

3 Rackheath in Norfolk — a late-stage replacement for Coltishall — considered the most sustainable site in the CPRE survey.

4 Northwest of Bicester in Oxfordshire — a site shift from the strongly opposed Weston Otmoor.

Note that Rossington near Doncaster and northeast Elsenham in Essex are earmarked for a second wave.

CPRE evaluated the sustainability of all the 15 sites on the shortlist and found them wanting on a huge range of criteria. Some of these were environmental issues, such

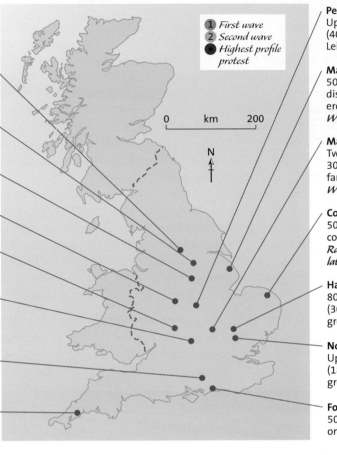

Leeds City Region
Sites sought in former coal-mining district of Selby

Rossington ②
Up to 15 000 homes, brownfield site

Rushcliffe
Near Nottingham

Curborough
5500 homes on brownfield site
Withdrawn

Middle Quinton ⊛
6000 homes on old army depot

Weston Otmoor ⊛
10 000–15 000 homes, many low cost. Loss of wildlife
Revised location northwest of Bicester ①

Whitehill-Bordon ①
5500 homes (2000 low cost) on MoD land. Loss of wildlife

St Austell (Imerys) ①
5000 homes on former china clay mines

① *First wave*
② *Second wave*
⊛ *Highest profile protest*

0   km   200

N
↑

Pennbury ⊛
Up to 15 000 homes, (4000 low cost) near Leicester

Manby
5000 homes for people displaced by coastal erosion
Withdrawn

Marston
Two schemes. Up to 30 000 homes. Loss of farmland and villages
Withdrawn

Coltishall
5000 homes (2000 low cost) on former airfield
Rackheath, Norfolk: a late-stage replacement ①

Hanley Grange
8000 homes (3000 low cost) on greenfield site

Northeast Elsenham ②
Up to 5000 homes (1800 low cost) on greenfield site

Ford
5000 homes, partly on old airfield

Figure 4.3
The proposed location of eco-towns in the UK, July 2009

as being built on high-quality rural land or in areas of high flood risk, or incorporating substantial areas of greenfield land, often attractive country of high ecological value. Of even greater concern was that these towns were not designed to be self-sufficient, which would lead to problems of transport provision. Increase in car use for employment and shopping would clearly add to the carbon footprint. In many sites local people and councils were fiercely opposed to their designation: for example, so well-orchestrated was the campaign against Weston Otmoor that the proposed site was shifted 10 miles away to the northwest of Bicester. A further controversy was that building large numbers of houses in pleasant rural areas was seen as completely unsustainable; the emphasis on up to 30% affordables provoked fear of 'green ghettos' being developed, especially if residents had no access to jobs locally. Not even the professional town planning bodies could agree whether eco-towns would be truly sustainable.

So here is a top-down government scheme, with many green credentials, hopefully scoring top marks for environmental sustainability, but certainly not 'ticking all the boxes' for socio-economic sustainability. Some of the eco-town sustainability objectives are incompatible with each other — notably building large estates of affordable houses with related industrial development while maintaining the quality of the rural environment and meeting the desire to manage climate change.

For further research, do an online search for the report *Eco-towns: Living a Greener Future*.

12

Using case studies

(a) Draw up a table to summarise the arguments for and against building eco-towns in rural England.

(b) Research the four chosen first-wave sites on the internet to consider why CPRE has described them as 'the least worst options'.

Guidance

(a) The arguments for will include environmental advantages such as climate change mitigation. Against will be issues of socio-economic sustainability and particular site-based issues.

(b) Research is likely to show the following:

(i) Rackheath — results of favourable CPRE report as the most sustainable site. Concerns over congestion around Norwich.

(ii) Imerys China Clay Community — chronic poverty of central Cornwall, dereliction of china clay from mine-working. Lack of rural employment and affordable housing.

(iii) Whitehill Bordon — might emphasise high percentage of low-grade and brownfield land and compatibility with local and regional planning objectives, already built-up nature of area (8000 ex-MoD homes) and also low levels of local opposition, although it is also close to the new South Downs National Park.

(iv) Northwest of Bicester, Oxfordshire is a new site, much better than the hugely contested Weston Otmoor (98% greenfield site, SSSIs, green belt etc.). There is a huge demand for affordable housing in the area and the plans are very attractive, with homes among allotments, parks and playing fields. The transport infrastructure exists, albeit currently overstretched. Could be seen as a growth corridor. Water and sewerage systems are already overstretched.

Sustainable development of provision in developed areas

If you look back to the section on changing service provision (page 31) you might envisage the following scenario, which could be termed 'So is it goodbye to the rural idyll?':

- non-existent public transport
- village school about to close
- post office under threat
- no chance of buying a house
- pub boarded up
- village doctor fighting a campaign to keep the rural pharmacy
- increasing isolation and social exclusion for the young, the poor and the old — the 'carless society'
- only low-paid, often seasonal jobs
- almost total dependence on the nearby market town for meeting daily basic needs — a 20-km round trip just for petrol

Rural deprivation is the state of lacking the essentials for a decent quality of life in a rural area. As Figure 4.4 shows, in England the picture is of pockets of severe deprivation among general rural prosperity.

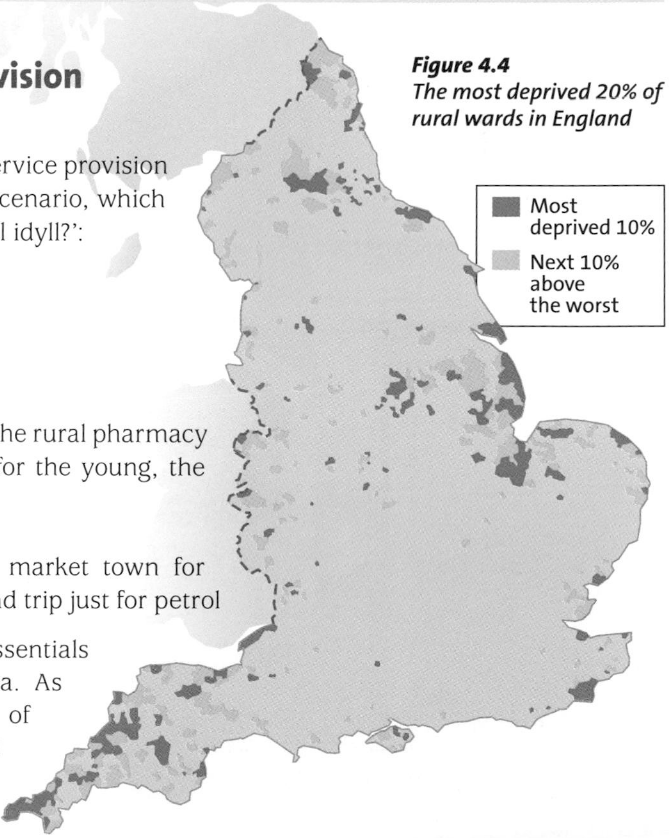

Figure 4.4
The most deprived 20% of rural wards in England

■ Most deprived 10%
■ Next 10% above the worst

One of the key ways to improve the quality of life of the rural disadvantaged is for the government to facilitate, by pump-priming, sustainable and innovative solutions to service provision developed by the village communities themselves. In England, as in many other developed countries, there are a number of programmes by which rural communities are grant-aided to do this. These include the **Vital Villages programme**, which funds:

■ Parish Plan Grants, to help communities identify the social, economic and environmental issues facing their village
■ Rural Transport Partnerships, which aim to ease mobility deprivation by funding innovative schemes such as car clubs, car sharing, dial-a-ride, and community taxi and minibus schemes
■ Community Services Grants, to help communities maintain or introduce services that are local priorities, for example a community village shop, community-based childcare schemes, often based at local schools, or community-based IT hubs such as the one in Shilbottle, Northumberland

Figure 4.5
Community services in rural areas such as access to a cash machine and IT facilities, are often provided by the village shop

Millennium Grants were also available for funding village halls and community centres, which have the capacity to develop into multi-use outlets. Partnership working is very successful in funding schemes for affordable houses within small-scale brownfield sites in villages. A further solution is the provision of outreach services, whereby mobile post offices, banks, cinema, libraries, hairdressers, fish vans etc. make up any deficits in services in order to overcome opportunity deprivation.

In the Scottish Islands there is even a mobile dentist service. Inevitably much of the provision is enhanced by the internet for a whole range of business services and also medical consultations, and networking for interest groups.

Other schemes are involved with employment: rural training centres provide localised skills training (e.g. the Aspire Centre at Burford, Shropshire, which specialises in engineering), while 'Wheels 2 Work' helps young people by providing them with mopeds or subsidised driving lessons to help them get to work. Other schemes provide grants for new rural enterprise start-ups, often in rural tourism (seen as the saviour of the countryside). Numerous schemes have reused redundant or derelict buildings for this purpose.

In many communities, villagers are striving to develop carbon-neutral communities and are developing sustainable schemes for recycling and energy use. There are examples of experimental rural eco-villages such as Crystal Waters in Queensland, Australia (based on permaculture), or West Harwood in West Lothian, based on lowland crofting. Many of these pioneering eco-villages have sustainable housing designs, sustainable energy programmes and sustainable waste

Contemporary Case Studies

management schemes (lots of composting!). A second type of future eco-village is one based on teleworking, such as Little River in South Island, New Zealand, whose professional inhabitants work on the internet as global researchers and promote sustainable living (food, water, energy). What is needed for success is a good community spirit with a critical mass of 'movers and shakers'.

A range of innovative solutions is summarised in Table 4.1.

Table 4.1
Innovative solutions in the Shropshire area

Services	The bad news: problems	The good news: innovative solutions
Food shops	Supermarkets opening even in quite small towns — lower prices, free buses Increased rural car ownership	Development of new types of shops Country stores and local farmers' market (Craven Arms) Parish/community shop (Waters Upton) Farm shops (24 in Shropshire) Garage shop (Tern Hill)
Post offices	Small offices downgraded to part-time — unattractive for people to buy Government strategies divert pensions business to banks	Post offices in pubs, churches etc. New deals for rural post offices with banks Expansion of business, e.g. photocopying, cards, stationery, IT services, cleaners (Shawbury)
Public transport	Bus deregulation led to closure of uneconomic routes Rising car ownership — limits passengers to young and very old Local government/councils lack funds	Grants for community taxis, dial-a-ride and quality bus partnership (Shropshire) 'Wheels 2 work' (moped scheme) for young workers (south Shropshire)
Village schools and libraries	Ageing population leads to a lack of customers Many schools are very small and expensive to run (under 50 pupils)	Development of rural nurseries, school clusters, mobile IT bus (North Shropshire Education Action Zone) Increased use of mobile libraries Improved government grants
Healthcare	Closure of GP branch surgeries and loss of district nurse services Decline of NHS dentistry Escalating NHS costs	Creation of mini health centres, development of rural pharmacies (Shawbury) Use of internet for consultations
Village halls	Changing family habits Withdrawal of youth clubs and social services	Millennium grants for refurbishment Reels on Wheels/Flicks in the Sticks mobile cinemas, Youth Bus, which tours villages

In conclusion, in order to achieve a sustainable future what is needed is joined-up thinking by governments (national and local) to ensure that their diverse initiatives are linked as part of an overall vision, and that one action such as developing internet services does not impact on the viability of other providers such as post offices. Equally, much of the funding is short-term and time-constrained, and much longer-term commitment is needed to achieve sustainability.

In south Shropshire, for example, piecemeal development has led to a mosaic of sustainable schemes which fail to provide a unified package. Some are inevitably experimental, and close because of withdrawal of funding.

While there are many difficulties, there are also numerous examples of bottom-up success, where a rural community becomes sufficiently dynamic to reverse its decline. Research Allenheads in Northumberland as an example. The village has, internally, been brought back from terminal decline by its community.

The role of sustainability in developing areas

There is a near-universal consensus that the critical development challenge confronting many developing rural areas — especially in sub-Saharan Africa and south Asia — is the reduction of poverty and the need to improve the well-being of the rural poor, 70% of whom are subsistence farmers. Poverty in sub-Saharan Africa is actually growing, whether it be measured by a figure such as less than $2 a day to live on or by an index of capability deprivation which looks at lack of access to the basics for a good quality of life: food, water, health, education and infrastructure. It is not only very severe but also very widespread, exacerbated by external shocks such as short-term climate change and natural disasters, conflicts, spread of diseases such as HIV/AIDS, TB and malaria, and the global credit crunch. These vulnerable people also face stresses caused by fluctuating world prices for crops, environmental degradation, famine and food insecurity, and water poverty.

Figure 4.6
The poverty and environment connection

Rural poverty can be tackled on a number of scales. At a macro level there are policies to attempt to create a more level playing field for world trade, and to develop

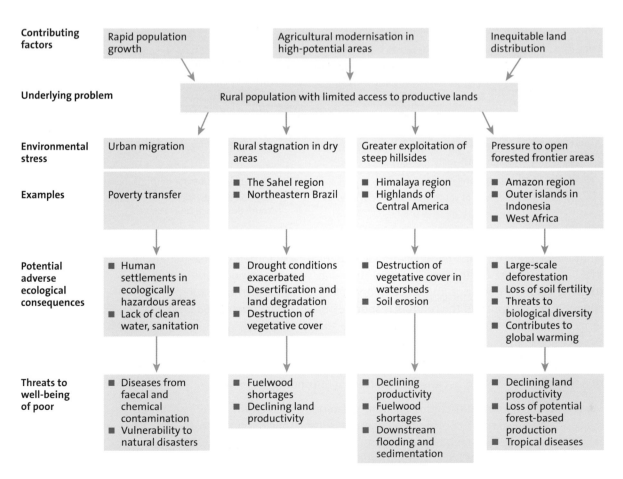

Contributing factors	Rapid population growth		Agricultural modernisation in high-potential areas		Inequitable land distribution
Underlying problem		Rural population with limited access to productive lands			
Environmental stress	Urban migration	Rural stagnation in dry areas	Greater exploitation of steep hillsides	Pressure to open forested frontier areas	
Examples	Poverty transfer	■ The Sahel region ■ Northeastern Brazil	■ Himalaya region ■ Highlands of Central America	■ Amazon region ■ Outer islands in Indonesia ■ West Africa	
Potential adverse ecological consequences	■ Human settlements in ecologically hazardous areas ■ Lack of clean water, sanitation	■ Drought conditions exacerbated ■ Desertification and land degradation ■ Destruction of vegetative cover	■ Destruction of vegetative cover in watersheds ■ Soil erosion	■ Large-scale deforestation ■ Loss of soil fertility ■ Threats to biological diversity ■ Contributes to global warming	
Threats to well-being of poor	■ Diseases from faecal and chemical contamination ■ Vulnerability to natural disasters	■ Fuelwood shortages ■ Declining land productivity	■ Declining productivity ■ Fuelwood shortages ■ Downstream flooding and sedimentation	■ Declining land productivity ■ Loss of potential forest-based production ■ Tropical diseases	

Contemporary Case Studies

appropriate aid and debt relief strategies for the least developed countries. At a more micro level both governments and NGOs are spearheading a combination of top-down and bottom-up strategies to tackle the complex interrelated problems of environmental degradation and poverty. The Vietnam case study (*Case study 11*) shows top-down strategies, and the work of ASAP in Burkina Faso (*Case study 12*) shows bottom-up strategies, both of which have stemmed out-migration and improved rural quality of life.

Figure 4.6 shows how poverty and environmental degradation are interlinked and lead to an unsustainable situation.

At the heart of the rural poverty issue and the need to provide a secure future is low agricultural production leading to food insecurity. A cocktail of factors has caused this, including: very strong population growth (families often consist of eight members); poor state of the infrastructure which is needed to link producers, processors and consumers; unfair trading conditions and fluctuating prices; widespread morbidity that lowers agricultural work rates; land tenure issues and persistent instability from disasters and wars.

Many NGOs have been highly successful in working with local communities in rural areas. You could research examples such as WaterAid, ActionAid, Tearfund, Oxfam or Christian Aid. Their projects are not only involved with agriculture but also lay the foundations for the development of the rural non-agricultural sector by:

- investing in primary schooling and rural health programmes
- increasing rural public works such as mini-dams, mini-hydros and solar energy schemes using appropriate technology
- investing in links to external markets via ICT programmes
- establishing microfinance, e.g. the AMINA programme developed by the African Development Fund in ten countries of Africa, which aims to help micro-entrepreneurs in a way similar to the pioneering work of the Grameen Bank in Bangladesh (**www.afdb.org**)

The two case studies that follow look at how FARM-Africa has helped very poor rural African farmers and herders by providing practical help to ensure food security for their families, and how in Tanzania's Udzungwa National Park all-round sustainable development strategies operate to safeguard the biodiversity and at the same time enhance the socio-economic futures of the people.

FARM-AFRICA

Case study 24

FARM-Africa is a UK- and African-based NGO, developed and supported by farming communities in the UK. Its aims are threefold:

- to save lives in Africa, and to improve the quality of life for Africa's farming families and communities
- to provide practical help so that farmers and herders can provide more food for their families and ensure future generations do not have to depend on aid
- to combine research and training in order to develop expertise that can be passed on to organisations and individuals throughout Africa, by working directly with African farmers

The work takes place in remote rural areas with poor communities who have little or no access to agricultural research. FARM-Africa works alongside local farmers, to listen to their needs and identify problems limiting agricultural production. It then seeks to find sustainable solutions, often applying intermediate technology to issues such as pest control, treatment of livestock diseases, or soil and water conservation. Other projects are involved in empowering local women through dairy goat projects, and helping local schoolchildren to develop farming skills. FARM-Africa passes on learning from projects to local people so they can develop their capacity to do such tasks as rudimentary veterinary care or building mini-dam for seasonal river diversions, so that the benefits will continue long after the NGO has moved on to a new area.

13

Using case studies

Research the website www.farmafrica.org.uk. Explain how FARM-Africa's projects could be considered to be sustainable.

Guidance

Refer back to the sustainability quadrant (Figure 4.2) as a framework and use this to structure your answer.

FARM-Africa's projects have been criticised by some because of their small scale and their failure to make agricultural production more intensive. Such intensive production would lead to potential for cash cropping. The Green Revolution certainly increased productivity in both southern Asia and Latin America, and it has been asked whether Africa needs a similar revolution, or indeed could cope with one.

CGIAR (the Consultative Group on International Agriculture Research) can be a powerful force for achieving sustainable development in agriculture. Its research (40% of its funding is invested in Africa) has led to:
- the development of many new varieties of maize and rice that have higher yields even when grown in difficult conditions (drought and low-fertility soil)
- integrated pest management by the biological control of pests in crops such as cassava
- more sustainable ways of using irrigation, which is often too costly for many peasant farmers

The Alliance for a Green Revolution in Africa (AGRA), an organisation funded by several US donors such as the Bill & Melinda Gates Foundation and the Rockefeller Foundation, has had some success, for example with Nerica rice, which has a short growing cycle, resists weeds and therefore gives double yields. Current research is focused on developing drought-resistant varieties of cassava, maize and millet, which will help farmers cope with climate change.

The big problem with the Green Revolution in Asia was that the HYV varieties required far greater inputs such as irrigation water, fertilisers and pesticides, all of which would be too costly for peasant farmers in Africa to purchase — thus it could be seen as unsustainable.

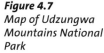
A further issue in many parts of Africa is the need to develop supporting technologies to ensure farmers can store the surpluses and sell their products on. Elsewhere, where TNCs have developed areas for cash cropping, often on high-quality land, peasant farmers have been pushed towards less favourable areas, which again has contributed to lower yields and may challenge the notion of a successful 'greening of Africa'.

UDZUNGWA MOUNTAINS NATIONAL PARK

Case study 25

The Udzungwa Mountains area in central Tanzania has been dubbed 'Africa's ark'. Not only is the rainforest in pristine condition (a rarity for the African continent) and a biodiversity eco region (WWF Global 200), but it also contains the highest concentration of endemic species in the world. It was for this reason designated as Tanzania's twelfth national park in 1992.

As with all Tanzanian national parks, the aims are to conserve the biodiversity of the rainforest while at the same time managing an effective community-based development programme that promotes sustainable livelihoods for the local people. In Udzungwa the issues are complex, as over 60 000 people live in a series of villages in a confined belt of land running parallel to the eastern edge of the park. These villages have traditionally relied on the forest for hunting and fuelwood. The former activity is now banned and only manual fuelwood gathering is allowed on just two days a week. It was clearly up to the park authorities (TANAPA) to establish means of community consultation and involvement, as initially relationships between villagers and park rangers were very strained. Therefore a number of projects to develop sustainable livelihoods for the local people were launched.

Figure 4.7
Map of Udzungwa Mountains National Park

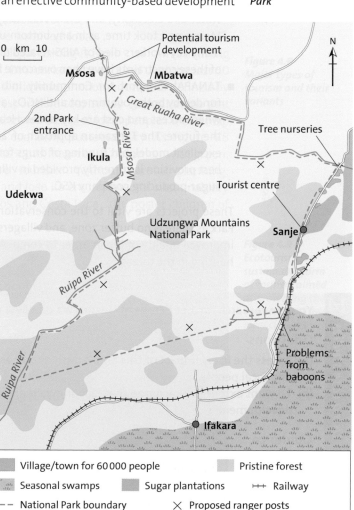

- WWF has developed tree nurseries and agro-forestry in nearly all the villages, which the local communities are being trained to manage — these will supply timber and fuelwood, and the tree crops provide an additional source of income.
- TANAPA has developed an ecotourist project, with tourist facilities being concentrated at the park headquarters at Sanje. The knowledge

Real ecotourism has the following seven characteristics, as defined by Martha Honey:

- It involves travel to natural destinations: these destinations are noted for their geodiversity and biodiversity and are usually under some kind of environmental protection, such as national park status. While some are remote wilderness areas, e.g. Antarctica, others are the homes of indigenous people. Many ecotourist operations, e.g. in Tanzania or Uganda, are built around systems of national parks.

- It strives to minimise the impact on the environment through appropriate design and operation of facilities (eco-hotels) or using zoning to manage the carrying capacity in order to limit damage to the ecosystems. This strategy is very successfully employed in the Galapagos. One controversial issue is trophy hunting for big game within conservation areas. This was originally associated with Zimbabwe's CAMPFIRE project, but is increasingly a feature of many African game parks that are extractive reserves. The theory is that animals are hunted at a sustainable rate (they are a renewable resource), and so the balance of the ecosystem is conserved.

- It builds environmental awareness, by educating both local people and tourists. Cruises to areas such as Antarctica are run on the Lindblad plan, with education about the wildlife and scenery during the trip, but one concern is that not all would-be ecotourists want this model. Well-trained, multilingual naturalist guides are therefore an essential investment, as is education of the local people, especially school children, who can enjoy free local trips. In many cases, as in Udzungwa National Park, the indigenous people have outstanding knowledge that needs to be harnessed as part of the ecotourism development.

- It provides direct financial benefits for conservation: charging admission fees to national parks and taxing tour companies and airline passengers on arrival or departure generates revenue for conservation. For example, in the Bwindi reserve in Uganda, gorilla-viewing fees are charged by the hour ($150+), so the conservation work in the park is self-supporting and development programmes have been funded in communities adjacent to the park. At the same time agreements have been made with the communities for limited harvesting of medicinal plants and honey as a further source of income, thus reinforcing the sustainability of the project.

- It provides financial benefits and empowerment for local people: ecotourism will only be successful if there are 'happy people' in the areas affected. Many parks have buffer zones around their edge (for example, Korup National Park in Cameroon), where certain controlled activities such as fuelwood gathering and hunting can take place around tribal villages. Udzungwa in Tanzania, however, offers a different picture: it has no buffer zone, and a large number of rapidly growing villages are crammed in between the park and the sugar estates (Figure 4.7). For this reason a range of sustainable developments (*Case study 25*) is vital, in order not only to conserve the pristine rainforest ecosystem but also to help the local population out of poverty. So successful has been the creation of wealth in the Galapagos, compared with the rest of Ecuador, that there has been unsustainable growth in immigration from the Ecuador mainland.

If ecotourism is to be viewed as a successful tool for rural development, the control must be in the hands of the local communities or villages (a bottom-up scheme).

NGOs such as WWF (in Udzungwa) or Conservation International (CI) ensure this is a feature of dozens of ecotourism projects in biodiversity hotspots (areas of high biodiversity under great threat).

■ Ecotourism respects local culture: in areas such as the Galapagos and Antarctica there are no local cultures, but in many areas there are indigenous peoples whose cultures are very vulnerable to dilution, especially where the communities are small and isolated. Governments in the Maldives and Zanzibar, both Islamic societies, are very concerned to manage the behaviour of tourists. In theory, ecotourists respect dress codes and local customs, but this is not always the case, as it depends on educating individuals. An example of inappropriate ecotourism is the case of an American company which offered jungle treks in Papua New Guinea to search out uncontacted tribes who had never seen outsiders!

■ Ecotourism supports human rights and democratic movements: in post-apartheid South Africa ecotourism and cultural tourism are both promoted as the country's passport to international acceptance and respectability. Interestingly, in Ecuador an ecotourism initiative by the Quechua people — running ecotours in the rainforest of the Napo region — was so successful that the national government banned the enterprise because it considered the tribes were not contributing enough taxes and were becoming 'too independent'.

Ecotourism is clearly a successful sustainable approach that can deliver the 'triple whammy' of environmental, socio-cultural and economic benefits.

A study of Costa Rica shows that when ecotourism develops into mass tourism (and it has seen an average 20% annual rise in numbers since 1990), it has to be very carefully managed. Costa Rica's highly successful tourism industry is now built around four 'brands': adventure, 'sun, sand and sea', rural community-based homestays, and ecotourism itself, with a drive for high quality in each area. So far the strategy seems to be working.

The role of technology in developing rural areas

Technology consists of tools, systems, processes and structures invented by humans that allow them to manage their environment more effectively and to satisfy their human needs. Rural lives can be transformed by technologies for increasing food and water security, for raising standards of health and sanitation, for creating and saving energy, for improving levels of income, and for overcoming isolation by improved communications.

In particular ICT can break down barriers to knowledge by delivering information on health or education matters. It also breaks down barriers to participation, for example by displaying details of job availability, or market prices for farmers and traders, or legal rights for citizens. ICT can also remove barriers to economic opportunity by allowing people to telework in remote rural areas, thus diversifying employment, or allowing them to manage their finances without visiting a bank.

It also helps to overcome their social exclusion and isolation by allowing them to network with the wider world.

While technology has been vital in arresting the spiral of decline in remote rural areas in developed countries, it is in developing rural areas that technology has had the most dramatic impact in recent years. A digital divide still exists, but the process of leapfrogging is revolutionising rural life in a number of ways. Technological leapfrogging is the process by which poor rural areas are able to access the latest digital technology by 'jumping over' unfair, less efficient and more expensive twentieth-century technology such as land lines or expensive electricity transmission lines, instead using wireless modes such as mobile phone masts, satellite technology and solar power systems, which can be built very quickly and almost anywhere in the world.

The following selection of case studies will explore how computers and the broadband revolution and mobile phones have transformed the quality of life of millions of people, lifting them out of poverty.

Computers and the broadband revolution

Even with the plans to build new transcontinental fibre optic cables, such as the Eastern Africa Submarine Cable System (EASSy), and the development of turnkey satellite links to many village centres, schools and universities that are now affordable given the availability of an initial setup grant, the high cost of computers and software represents a serious impediment to individual access. Basic computers such as the XO and the Simputer have been developed, along with stripped-down software, promising to deliver low-cost individual computing to developing countries. In Africa, however, IT expansion is hampered by pirated software and super-slow load times, which means that PC viruses are pandemic and very hard to eradicate. This is a major problem in Ethiopia, which has enthusiastically embraced IT yet suffered major data losses.

Case study 26 shows how computers are transforming rural lives in India, and *Case study 27* illustrates how computers can reach the most remote places on Earth.

Case study 26 **RURAL INDIA ONLINE**

For many people in developing countries the cheapest computer is still too expensive. Also, a significant number of villagers cannot read and write and therefore find it difficult to use the internet. To overcome these barriers the Indian Institute of Science in Bangalore and a locally based software company, Encore, have designed a low-cost handheld computer. Their simple computer, or Simputer, provides internet and e-mail access in local languages with touch screen and microbanking functions. Future versions will have speech recognition and text-to-speech software for users with low literacy levels.

The Indian government is looking at the possibility of buying and distributing these machines at village and district levels so that each small community has at least five Simputers. Then, each villager will only have to buy a smart card, which costs anything between 50 and 100 rupees ($1 to $2). They will be able to store all their internet and e-mail preferences etc. on the card and rent the machines for 20 cents an hour. The villagers can use them for other purposes as well, such as microcredit facilities, and storing and accessing agricultural data. Simputers are adaptable to a large range of rural applications. With a special smart card, they can also be used to collect village census and agricultural data and for routine services such as railway ticket reservations.

The e-Gram Suraj project uses the Simputer device to store and pass on important information. The project has been introduced in the Dongargaon and Kurd villages and it is the first Hindi-based system to be used in the area. It provides almost all information about a village — population, families, water resources, human resources, land etc. It uses a touch screen and can also be used to update local information that can then be analysed across villages.

In the Chhattisgarh project teachers use their experience and creativity to create content for the Simputers using a school computer. Examples include a geography quiz, a Hindi-to-English dictionary, and a basketball game to help children understand projectile motion. They then transfer the content to the Simputers. This activity in itself encourages the teachers to feel more comfortable with using technology. In the project there was one Simputer for every five children. Children use the Simputers in class, with guidance from the teachers. At the end of each day the computers are placed back in the school library.

THE BROADBAND REVOLUTION REACHES MONGOLIA

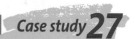
Case study 27

Mongolia has a very sparsely distributed population, the average GDP is equivalent to £1360 and more than a third of the people live in poverty, yet it has a literacy rate of 96%. Forty per cent of the population are nomadic herders living in 'gers' (nomadic tents), just as they did 1000 years ago. In addition, Mongolia has a poor infrastructure (the telephone density is 4.1 and radio density is 15.7 per 100 inhabitants), so traditional media cannot reach more than a small proportion of the population. This makes the use of the internet a worthwhile development, but the cost is a problem. The Asia–Pacific Development Information Programme (APDIP), a United Nations-funded organisation, has developed Citizen Information Service Centres (CISCs). The project, which started in 1999, set up computer workstations, a printer and a small library with reference material. The services of the CISCs are free. They also serve as training centres, where visitors can learn basic computer skills and get help taking their first steps in the internet world. People living in remote rural areas, including in parts of the Gobi desert, can now connect to the central government, apply for grants online, receive news online, and obtain basic training in computing. For example, Mongolian steppe nomads have access to information about weather and commodity prices by means of a 'Cyber Ger'. The programme's long-term aim is to encourage businesses and colleges to use IT and to develop a culture of open information.

Mobile phones take the world by storm

A UN report in 2009 revealed the speed and scale of the world's love of mobile phones and the breathtaking growth of mobile phone technology. Africa is currently the continent with the fastest growth, with penetration soaring from just one in 50 people in 2000 to around 30% in 2009. Developing countries now account for two-fifths of the use.

Mobile phones can play a significant part in promoting bottom-up socio-economic development, even among the poorest rural communities. Access to mobile telecommunications in developing countries can help bridge the digital divide. Mobiles do not require the same levels of education and literacy as other new technologies such as computers or the internet. This makes them more accessible. Accessibility is further increased by the lower up-front expenditure. The rapid spread of mobiles has been aided by pre-pay options that allow users to control their spending. The number of mobile users is often much higher than the actual number of phones, as many people allow family and friends to use their phones, and in some countries there are shared phone initiatives, e.g. Grameenphone in Bangladesh and the Uganda Village Phone Initiative.

Much of the take-up is thought to have been driven by the money transfer services that allow people without bank accounts to send money speedily and safely by text message, which the recipient — typically a family member — can cash at the other end. An example is Vodafone's M-Pesa money transfer system in Kenya, which was launched in 2007 and now has 5.5 million users.

Fig 4.10
Village phones, Uganda

Charles Sturge/Alamy

There are numerous other vital applications which help rural development: for example, in rural Rwanda 'barefoot' healthcare workers use mobile phones to enter vital data, order drugs and consult senior specialists. In the remote Andes, women's knitting and weaving cooperatives use mobile phone technology to access fashion designs and colours for the season in order to ensure maximum sales. Smart phones are now available, usually at a village level in the cybercafé or owned by an entrepreneur. The possibilities are endless.

Case study **28** — MOBILE PHONE USE IN SOUTH AFRICA

In Kenya, Safaricom has introduced a text messaging service. The Sokoni service transmits daily reports from the Kenya Agricultural Commodity Exchange (KACE). Users simply text the name of the commodity they are interested in, such as 'maize' or 'sheep', and receive an instant reply with an update on its price that morning at each market. This enables them to assess the best place and time to buy or sell. The service also allows traders to offer their goods for sale or to place bids, as well as to post short messages or agricultural questions.

The South African company Vodacom has introduced more than 24 000 community phones into poor, rural and under-serviced areas where there are few or no fixed-line

Figure 4.11
A mobile phone shop in South Africa

TopFoto

phones. These enable customers to pay by the call and provide access to telecommunications for people who cannot afford their own phone. Community phones are run by local businesses as phone shops, under franchise. Vodacom provides business training and support to franchisees to help them make their business a success. Around 5000 community phone shops have been established, either housed in customised shipping containers or, for example, as part of Spaza shops (small grocery stores in the country).

Phone shops are also bringing additional benefits. More than 20 000 jobs have been created, and the shops help attract many other businesses, boosting local economies. In addition, the franchise system adopted by Vodacom is helping to empower black entrepreneurs and women, with around 40% of franchises held by women.

Increased use of mobile phones also improves access to information. Knowledge of latest prices in different markets, for example, can improve price transparency for small farmers and fishermen who can cut out the middleman and gain direct access to markets.

Recent research studies completed by Vodafone, which owns a majority stake in Vodacom, on the socio-economic impact of mobiles in South Africa found the following:

- The value of mobile phones to the individual is greater because other forms of communication (such as postal systems, roads and fixed-line phones) are often poor. Mobiles provide a point of contact and enable users to participate in the economic system.
- Many people who cannot afford to own a mobile themselves can access mobile services through informal sharing with family and friends or through community phone shops, e.g. Grameenphone.
- Use of text messaging in rural communities is much lower, because of illiteracy and the many indigenous languages. This has implications for other technologies that use the written word, such as the internet.
- Mobiles have a positive and significant impact on economic growth and direct investment in an area. This impact may be twice as large in developing countries.

Rural Development & the Countryside

- A developing country with an extra ten phones per 100 people between 1996 and 2003 would have GDP growth 0.59% higher than an otherwise identical country.
- Eighty-five per cent of those surveyed in Tanzania and 79% in South Africa said they had more contact and better relationships with family and friends thanks to mobile phones.

Case study 29 — MUKEBA'S STORY

Mukeba's story shows how the acquisition of a mobile phone has revolutionised the life of one young African and the town he lives in — disaster-stricken Goma in the Democratic Republic of Congo (Figure 4.12).

From Congo to Kathmandu

How mobiles have transformed the world

Chris McGreal

For much of his life, Mukeba didn't have an address. His corrugated iron house had no number and his volcanic ash street in the heart of Goma had no name. There was no postal service and the phone system had long since disintegrated. So when his mother died in 1995 on the other side of the Democratic Rupublic of Congo, her church sent a note marked only 'Deograsias Mukuba, Goma'. Remarkably it got to him — but three weeks after the funeral.

That was before. Now Mukeba's address goes with him everywhere. It has transformed the 33-year-old's life. It is an old Nokia mobile phone. 'It was very hard discovering my mother had died and been buried and I didn't know anything about it for weeks,' said Mukeba. But that's how life was. If you lived in Goma, Kinshasa was another planet.

'I didn't really have any work. When the cell phones came I found the money and bought one because it was cool to have. It cost me $25 (£18). It's a lot.

'My brother lives in Kinshasa where he is a trader. He called me and asked me to start finding some things for him that you couldn't get in Kinshasa but you could find in Rwanda and Uganda, like some electrics and car parts. Now I speak to him every day. I send a lot of stuff. Now we are making money.'

Mobile phones have changed Congo irrevocably, especially Goma.

Now traders shipping imports to distant towns, farmers sending produce to the main cities, and those involved in the thriving gold and diamond smuggling trade use their phones to check prices, text quotes and arrange deliveries.

Women who once sold roasted corn by the roadside now make a living dealing in mobile top-up cards and recharging flat phone batteries in a town where much of the population doesn't have electricity.

'Everyone but the very poor has a cell phone,' said Mukeba. 'Even the guy who only makes a few dollars a day picking up passengers on his bike. Even the woman selling things by the roadside. Almost everyone finds the money.'

Cell phones have helped transform Goma in other ways. The town's economic boom of recent years has been fuelled by war and plunder, particularly of the rich mines in eastern Congo. Among them are diamonds and gold but also coltan, a rare but crucial element in mobile phones.

The small fortune to be made by mining it sent tens of thousands digging for black mud and attracted criminal syndicates and foreign armies. 'It all came at once,' said Mukeba. 'War, cell phones, dollars. Some people are getting very, very rich and everyone is making a little bit of money.'

© *Guardian* News and Media Ltd 2009

Figure 4.12
Extract from the Guardian, 3 March 2009

Many factors affect the spread of mobile phones:
- Economic factors — such as income per capita and the price of handsets and calls. Chinese models are very cheap and readily available in all African countries.
- Flexible use of appropriate business models — for example, smaller-value pre-pay top-up cards help overcome credit barriers and enable the use of mobiles as public telephones.
- Government policy — mobile phone use is higher in countries with more open telecommunications markets.
- Social and cultural factors — including urbanisation, women's empowerment and population density (which can affect the cost of deployment in rural areas).

In conclusion:

- ICT can help rural areas to develop, but the digital divide means that different solutions are appropriate for different countries.
- The successful introduction and use of ICT in rural areas is governed by a range of economic and social factors.
- There are many examples of the effective use of ICT to assist the development of rural areas in developing countries, but there are also many obstacles to be overcome.

15 Questions

Using case studies

(a) Explain what technologocal leapfrogging is. Use examples from the case studies to develop your definition.

(b) Outline the reasons why mobile phone technology has spread more rapidly than computer-based technology.

Guidelines

(b) The technology is cheaper, more user-friendly and easier to master. Note that with smart phones there is now an overlap, with multi-functions including internet access, and Chinese phones are now available very cheaply.

The other major thrust of technological leapfrogging is solar energy. Solar home systems are gradually spreading to many rural areas in the Indian subcontinent and other parts of the world. The technology costs are going down all the time, so government schemes are profiting. Typically a solar home system consists of an 80-watt solar panel, a charge controller, a battery, four compact fluorescent lamps, two LED lights, a 12-volt DC fan and a television socket. The solar panel charges the battery during daylight hours, then the stored energy powers home and street lighting, solar cooking stoves and, most importantly, a solar water disinfector.

One issue is the installation and maintenance of the solar technology. Both China and India have systems of barefoot solar engineers (frequently women) who have been taught the simple skills to demonstrate the value of solar energy for use in the home and in agriculture, health and enterprise operations.

In many villages in the African continent, NGOs such as Practical Action have installed solar-powered water pumps to provide a reliable source of clean water.

Rural rebranding in developed countries

The process of rebranding involves a combination of regeneration, in this case of a 'countryside in crisis', and reimaging in order to breathe new vitality into declining areas by positively changing their standing and reputation. The result, especially in rural areas in Europe, is to move from a landscape of crop and livestock production to a **post-productive countryside**. EU policy changes in agricultural practice and policy, known as the McSharry reforms, shifted the emphasis away from subsidies aimed at maximising yields and towards a more sustainable agriculture, where farmers are subsidised to be environmental stewards, conserving and protecting the landscape.

At the same time a second rebrand is taking place: a move towards a landscape of consumption based on rural tourism as the mainstay of the brand. This is a more widespread process, as rising amounts of leisure time, increasing disposable incomes, an ageing population with many active retired people, and almost universal access to a car have combined to promote the consumption of all types of rural landscape, not just 'high-value' national park areas with outstanding scenery, for leisure and tourism use. Counterurbanisation has resulted in increasing numbers of people living in the countryside or in rural–urban fringe areas who are seeking to use the nearby countryside for recreation. Equally, many urban dwellers seek the peace and tranquillity and the perceived freedom from stress of rural areas.

Figure 4.13
Challenges facing the UK countryside

Rural rebranding is especially buoyant in developed countries such as France, the USA, Canada, the UK and Australia, where it exists side by side with productive agriculture. Figure 4.13 summarises some of the challenges facing the UK countryside.

Lack of transport infrastructure – public transport may be infrequent and expensive. Car ownership is expensive

Agricultural change – low wages, mechanisation, cheaper imports and competition, high-profile diseases

Post-production transition – shift towards more sustainable agriculture has some farmers more reliant on a dwindling supply of government subsidies

Challenges for the countryside

Pockets of local depopulation – many communities have lost younger residents, forced out by uneven opportunity

Disappearance of rural services – the rationalisation of both private and public services in rural communities has been pronounced. This has had a significant impact on the nature, character and image of places

Issue of affordable housing – purchase of second homes by affluent urban-based middle-class householders. This form of gentrification inflates prices, excluding low-income would-be buyers

Changing rural economy – shift from production-based towards more service-oriented employment. There has been fragmentation of the local economy, creating uncertainties. Fewer guaranteed jobs

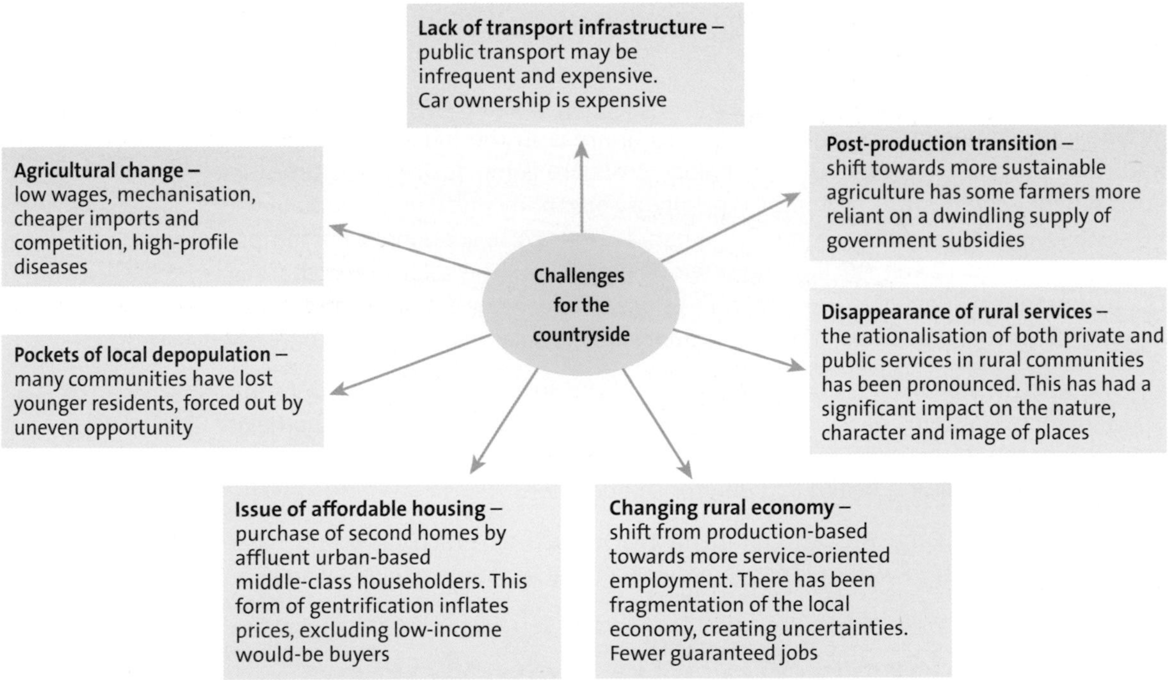

The traditional rural economy is based on primary activities: fishing, forestry, mining and quarrying and above all farming, which even in areas classified as extremely rural in the UK currently employs under 10% of people. Not only has there been a decrease in farming and farm-related employment, but also since the mid-1980s there has been a marked decline in farm incomes (1976: £5.5 billion; 2000: £1.88 billion (Source: DEFRA)).

This decline has had a knock-on effect on the whole rural economy. The factors that caused the farming crisis and the subsequent countryside crisis included:

Contemporary Case Studies

- falling prices resulting from cheaper imports (e.g. Danish bacon), aided by the strength of the pound (until 2008, when the pound weakened against the euro)
- the power of supermarkets, which drove down the price of milk and cereals (bread), while the cost of fuel, water for irrigation, fertilisers and credit increased
- increasingly unpredictable weather, as a result of climate change (autumn floods in 2000, summer floods in 2007–08, droughts in 2003 and late frosts in 2008–09)
- reforms to the Common Agricultural Policy (CAP), which meant that farmers were no longer guaranteed high prices
- major outbreaks of animal disease (in the 2001 foot and mouth outbreak it was estimated that £320 million of income and 7805 jobs were lost). In addition there were outbreaks of swine vesicular disease, bird flu, salmonella and BSE, which led to a fall in consumer confidence in British farm products. These diseases 'shut' whole swathes of countryside and had a knock-on impact far greater than that on farming itself

Table 4.2
Stewardship scheme in south Shropshire

Note that many of the factors that led to the post-productive revolution in farming have eased, with farm prices improving and supermarkets beginning to negotiate better deals for farmers after pressure from farm lobbying groups (e.g. the NFU), but the landscape of consumption has grown as farmers increasingly see the wisdom of diversification. Surveys in the Lake District and Snowdonia suggest that in up to 70% of farms diversification has become the main income generator. Moreover, many non-farm-based activities are independent of the original agricultural tradition.

The post-productive landscape results in a number of features, all of which are supported by grants and farm payments at a farm scale.

Environment-friendly farming

There used to be a movement towards extensification by means of set-aside payments, and also towards organic farming. However, in recent credit crunch times, farmers have become concerned that the market for high-cost organic produce is limited, and many are seeking redesignation to concentrate on high-quality but not strictly organic produce.

The set-aside schemes, which have become so important as havens for wildlife, are gradually being used again in response to rising farm prices and the threat of an impending global food crisis. Additionally, grants for **countryside**

Stewardship practice	Benefit
Cut half the hedges in alternate years	More berries for birds Benefits butterflies
Growing floristically enhanced strips on parts of farm	Benefits insects
Two field corners left to grow wild — half an acre each	Ensures greater biodiversity — habitats for a range of animals
Grass strips retained across slopes	Prevents surface erosion
Fifteen acres of brassicas planted after the corn crop	Feeds sheep through the winter and provides cover for wildlife
One hectare of wild seed cover sown	Provides shelter and feed for the birds throughout the year
Rough cultivation of four hectares of compulsory set-aside (drag cultivator through the soil)	Encourages lapwings to nest
Coppicing alder trees along the River Corve	Allows sunlight on the water, which benefits invertebrates and fish and helps control fungus which is killing the alders
Pollarding willow and fencing off the river to protect the alder so it can grow — but controlled grazing at times to keep down Himalayan balsam (an invasive alien species)	Protects alder to allow regeneration
Six-metre boundary by river where no spraying or spreading of fertiliser allowed	Protects river from pollution
Replanting lengths of hedges that have died off	Provides an important habitat and food source for birds; the headlands have wild flowers and provide a habitat for creatures such as voles

stewardship (Table 4.2) and the LEAF (Linking Environment and Farming) scheme have allowed farmers to develop and conserve hedgerows, wetlands and woodlands. Only in eastern England (the East Anglian prairies and the Fens) has the productive strand of the specialised, intensive, arable agribusiness continued.

Farm diversification

Figure 4.14 shows the huge range of diversification opportunities available. They can essentially be classified as farm-related (agricultural diversification) or off-farm (structural non-farm diversification). The farm-based activities, such as rearing new types of livestock (ostriches, llamas) or growing biofuels and other new crops, can have an impact on the landscape.

Figure 4.14
Farm diversification

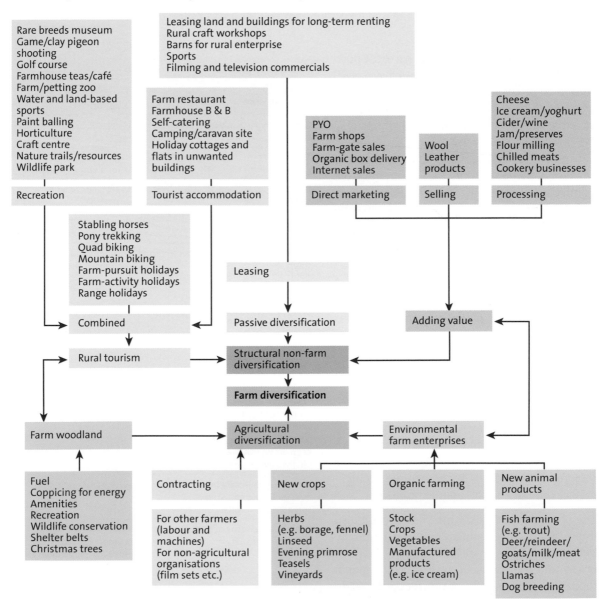

Many farms seek to add value to their farm products by specialising in quality farm-produced food that is sold locally (e.g. at farm shops and farmers' markets). Both the Red Tractor logo that symbolises quality British farming and the slogan 'Eat the view' have become widely known.

Other farmers develop activities that are transforming the countryside into a landscape of consumption. It is this second group that can be more controversial. A huge range of farm-based enterprises have been developed — the vast majority as tourist attractions. The Acton Scott working farm museum, for example, is focused on education and highly successful, with an additional boost from being featured in a television series, whereas others, such as Park Hall Farm in Shropshire, offer both educational experiences and entertainment. There are significant environmental implications for many of these larger-scale, more artificial developments, such as crowded rural roads, eroded hillsides, noise and light pollution. While they do provide considerable income opportunities for farmers and employment for local people, albeit of a part-time/seasonal nature, the environmental impacts are a downside. Think about some of the farm-based music festivals, such as Glastonbury. The picture of the UK countryside is therefore one of multi-functional activities, often, but not always, supporting each other. Figure 4.15 summarises how the impact of farm diversification can vary according to how 'alien' the activity is.

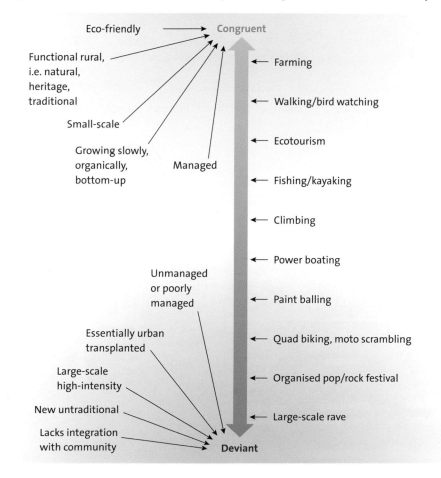

Figure 4.15
The impact of farm diversification

The degree of congruence varies with:
- the nature of the area — whether vulnerable or fragile or high-quality landscape/scenery
- the amount of carrying capacity
- the nature of visitors and their activities and behaviour
- the intensity of activity in space and over time
- the degree of management and its success

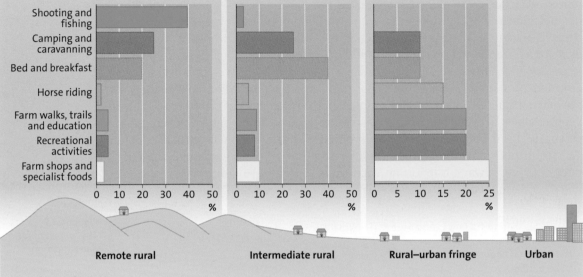

Source: Cameron Dunn

Figure 4.16
Nature of farm diversification in three different rural areas

As shown in Figure 4.16, the nature of the diversification is likely to vary with the location.

Figure 4.17
An example of farm diversification found in the rural–urban fringe area of Newcastle

Contemporary Case Studies

Rural rebranding

Rural rebranding can happen at a number of scales, and to be successful the marketing strategies need to be interlinked.

Rural tourism was traditionally concentrated in areas of outstanding scenery, such as the Lake District, or in historic market towns of national cultural significance, such as York, but there is increasing interest in both rural and heritage tourism generated by the media and effective marketing. All over the UK and elsewhere, groups of people (known as 'players') are involved in the development and marketing of places and areas as attractions for both day-visitors and tourists in order to attract income and provide employment. This is known as the **commodification** of the countryside.

Figure 4.18 summarises the stages in the rebranding of the countryside and shows which players are involved at the various stages. It is clearly logical to see a single attraction as part of the tourist strategy for the wider area — an approach known as piggy-back marketing. If the individual farm or village can be made part of a trail or tourist route, there are economies of scale to be made in terms of promotion. There is also evidence that the linked attractions offer a more diverse experience

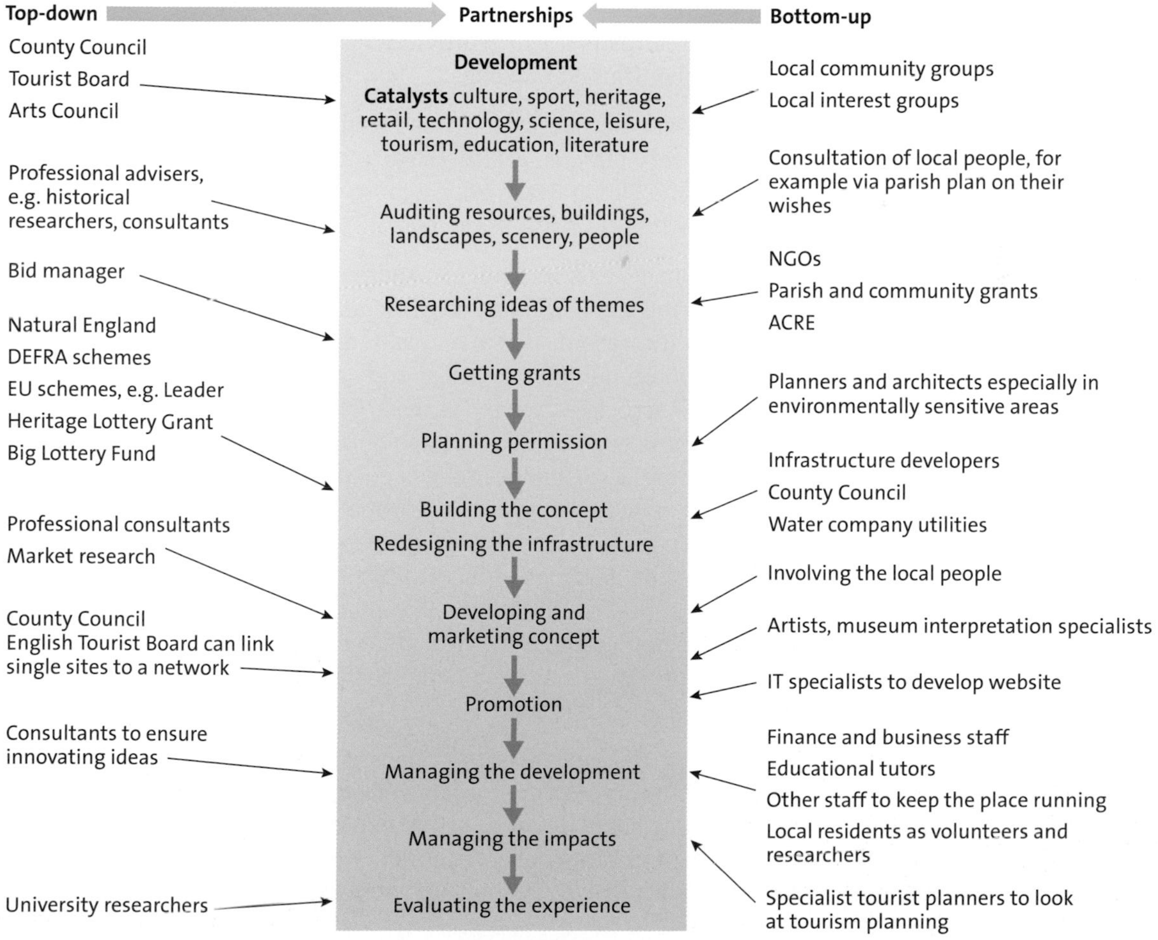

Figure 4.18
The players involved in the process of rural rebranding

Top-down   Partnerships   Bottom-up

County Council
Tourist Board
Arts Council

Professional advisers, e.g. historical researchers, consultants

Bid manager

Natural England
DEFRA schemes
EU schemes, e.g. Leader
Heritage Lottery Grant
Big Lottery Fund

Professional consultants
Market research

County Council
English Tourist Board can link single sites to a network

Consultants to ensure innovating ideas

University researchers

Development
Catalysts culture, sport, heritage, retail, technology, science, leisure, tourism, education, literature

Auditing resources, buildings, landscapes, scenery, people

Researching ideas of themes

Getting grants

Planning permission

Building the concept
Redesigning the infrastructure

Developing and marketing concept

Promotion

Managing the development

Managing the impacts

Evaluating the experience

Local community groups
Local interest groups

Consultation of local people, for example via parish plan on their wishes

NGOs
Parish and community grants
ACRE

Planners and architects especially in environmentally sensitive areas

Infrastructure developers
County Council
Water company utilities

Involving the local people

Artists, museum interpretation specialists

IT specialists to develop website

Finance and business staff
Educational tutors
Other staff to keep the place running

Local residents as volunteers and researchers

Specialist tourist planners to look at tourism planning

and therefore attract more visitors. It is also possible to achieve a larger carrying capacity, as the visitors can spread across a wider area in a number of sites. The use of festivals and special events is a good way of boosting visitor numbers across the year. Examples of these linked attractions include the following:

- Rail Ale Trails in Devon and Cornwall: these promote the sustainable use of five rural railway branch lines to enable people to enjoy the delights of traditional real ales in five rural pubs (and presumably stay in them) along the route. At the same time there are free souvenirs to collect and high-quality leaflets to 'help tourists have fun'.
- The Ribble Valley Food Trail in Lancashire: this links a number of quality local food-producing outlets such as farm shops, and restaurants and inns specialising in local food and local recipes.
- The Cider Route: this enables people to sample and learn about the variations in a local product — scrumpy and cider — to give them a reason for visiting a remote, not very well-known, yet beautiful area.
- Long-distance footpaths: routes such as the Pennine Way (noted for its overuse and footpath erosion), Offa's Dyke footpath or canal routes encourage people to extend their tour, stay along the route overnight and visit museums and shops, thus adding value to the local area.
- The Black and White Village Trail: centred on a series of 'magpie' villages, such as Eardisland in Herefordshire, which are noted for the style and appearance of their vernacular timber-framed buildings.

Sometimes the walk, river journey, cycle or road trail is themed around a particular person — sometimes very famous, e.g. the Elgar trail in the Malverns, sometimes almost unknown, e.g. the Simon Evans Way, a footpath in south Shropshire named after a local postman who was also a poet.

One way of linking attractions is to develop a theme for the whole area. There is a debate about whether the use of the tag 'country' actually promotes tourism in an area. It is designed to increase dispersal across a region, so that tourist revenues permeate to the maximum number of outlets and can link all the tourist offices in a region. This might be associated with:

- a symbol, e.g. Red Rose country (the heritage of Lancashire)
- a famous historic figure, e.g. Charles Dickens country in north Kent
- a fictional figure, as in Robin Hood country (not a great success as a name)
- a series of novels, e.g. Thomas Hardy's Wessex or Lorna Doone country in Exmoor, both given a boost by television productions
- a link to a television series, e.g. Last of the Summer Wine country in the Pennines
- a link to a film, e.g. Kettlewell, in the Yorkshire Dales, where the film *Calendar Girls* was shot. The film gave it a much-needed boost in overnight stays — in the bed where Dame Helen Mirren slept!

It is worth mentioning that not all promotions of rebrands are outstandingly successful. Sometimes the product is poorly conceived, or marketed on an inadequate budget, or the website is badly devised, or the exhibitions and interpretations are of poor quality, or there is simply oversaturation within the area. It may even be the name: the Secret Hills Discovery Centre is now the Shropshire Hills Discovery Centre.

While a link with a television series may have a limited lifespan, 'soaps' such as *Emmerdale* are long-running series and look to develop a tour to all the places where the episodes were filmed. Compo's Café from *Last of the Summer Wine*, in Holmfirth, is a similarly popular attraction. This can be very good business, especially if supported by appropriate souvenirs and even a theme park with viewing galleries showing the top episodes.

The ephemeral nature of this sort of tourism is well illustrated by Lyme Park, a National Trust property in Cheshire which included the renowned lake from which Colin Firth emerged as Mr Darcy in the television production of Jane Austen's *Pride and Prejudice* in 1995 — boosting visitors by over 50 000 in the following season. After 3 years visitors returned to the normal level, but even now special themed coach tours run.

Figure 4.19 shows some ways in which the success of rural rebranding can be assessed using a number of indicators, some of which can be surveyed using primary data.

Market towns that have undergone rebranding are the lifeblood of rural areas, as they provide the key services to their rural hinterlands, both for local people and visitors.

The positions of the market towns of Shropshire are shown in Figure 4.20. Some, e.g. Wem (home of the Eckford Sweet Pea) and Market Drayton (home of gingerbread), are struggling to maintain their unique characteristics and vibrancy, whereas others have been very successful in developing and adding value to their market town brand (market leader Ludlow).

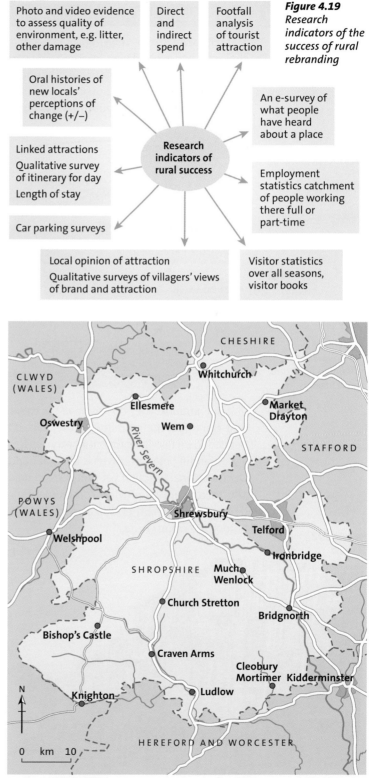

Figure 4.19 Research indicators of the success of rural rebranding

Research indicators of rural success

- Photo and video evidence to assess quality of environment, e.g. litter, other damage
- Direct and indirect spend
- Footfall analysis of tourist attraction
- Oral histories of new locals' perceptions of change (+/−)
- An e-survey of what people have heard about a place
- Linked attractions
  Qualitative survey of itinerary for day
  Length of stay
- Employment statistics catchment of people working there full or part-time
- Car parking surveys
- Local opinion of attraction
  Qualitative surveys of villagers' views of brand and attraction
- Visitor statistics over all seasons, visitor books

Figure 4.20 Map of Shropshire

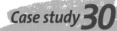

Case study 30 REBRANDING SOUTH SHROPSHIRE MARKET TOWNS

Market towns are a very important part of the south Shropshire landscape. Their character has evolved over hundreds of years, but as in other parts of England, choking fumes from traffic, bland new buildings not built from local stone (non-vernacular) and new superstores on the outskirts are all threatening them (CPRE). Even building a bypass can have a disastrous impact (Figure 4.21).

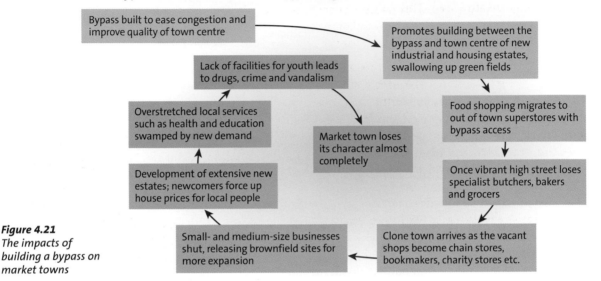

Figure 4.21
The impacts of building a bypass on market towns

Bypass built to ease congestion and improve quality of town centre → Promotes building between the bypass and town centre of new industrial and housing estates, swallowing up green fields → Food shopping migrates to out of town superstores with bypass access → Once vibrant high street loses specialist butchers, bakers and grocers → Clone town arrives as the vacant shops become chain stores, bookmakers, charity stores etc. → Small- and medium-size businesses shut, releasing brownfield sites for more expansion → Development of extensive new estates; newcomers force up house prices for local people → Overstretched local services such as health and education swamped by new demand → Lack of facilities for youth leads to drugs, crime and vandalism → Market town loses its character almost completely

It is a paradox: they do not have the capacity to cope with development, yet the lack of it can affect their vitality, as they fail to attract the injection of people and money needed to enable their essential services to survive.

Rebranding market towns is all about adding a new dimension that fits in well with the traditional function yet brings extra income, investment and people into the town. The towns aim to provide complementary strategies so that they do not compete directly with each other, and also to fit in with the general rural rebranding of the south Shropshire countryside.

Figure 4.22
Ludlow

Sue Warn

Ludlow: 'The town where you will be treated as a temporary resident'

Ludlow was the first 'Cittaslow' or slow town in the UK — it is a member of a growing international network of towns 'where the quality of life comes first'. Being 'slow' is an attitude that looks to preserve and promote quality and tradition (www. slowfood.org.uk, www.cittaslow.org.uk).

Ludlow is also a food town, so the bakers make the bread the old way, and farm animals are raised and butchered locally. Locals claim that the town of just 10 000 people has more Michelin stars per head than anywhere else in the world, other than Paris. It has pioneered the 'Local to Ludlow' brand (www.localtoludlow.org) with twice-monthly farmers' markets, farm tours and promotion of small local food businesses such as cheese and sweet making. An award-winning food centre is located just outside the town, where 80% of the food is locally sourced.

Ludlow is a festival town — examples include outdoor Shakespeare productions in the castle, a world famous food festival, art festivals, craft festivals, a green festival and a transport festival. It is a very important tourist town with its markets, castle, historic buildings and quality shops with traditional services. There is a range of specialist shops, from high-class clothes retailers to luxury food outlets, and many coffee shops and cafés. There is even an eco-park, with park and ride, to the east of the town.

Bishop's Castle: 'Refreshing in more ways than one'

Bishop's Castle is a small and ancient town surrounded by outstanding natural scenery, so it is an ideal touring centre, with quality pubs, self-catering cottages and coffee shops. Described as 'timeless yet buzzing', it has a selection of unusual shops and galleries selling batik, handmade crafts, real furniture, and second-hand books and vinyl records, as well as traditional cobblers and ironmongers.

There are numerous festivals, including the famous Real Ale Festival led by two local breweries, as well as Midsummer Rejoicing, Michaelmas Fair, Christmas lights, hunt meets and steam traction rallies. The town's rural industrial park, however, has experienced several closures, including those of trouser factories that could not compete in price with the far east, so manufacturing employment is limited.

Figure 4.23
Bishop's Castle

Bishop's Castle is working towards being a sustainable town. The award-winning 'Living Village' is a sustainable community of 30 houses (more planned) just minutes from the town centre. It is designed for people, not cars, with individual mixed-style eco-efficient houses (solar power, water recycling, wood-burning stoves, shared organic allotments etc.).

Church Stretton: 'In the heart of the Shropshire Hills'

Church Stretton lies in a rift valley between Long Mynd and Caer Caradoc within the Shropshire Hills AONB. It is an outdoor activities town with walking, horse riding, pony

Figure 4.24
Long Mynd

trekking, mountain biking, hang-gliding and gliding. It has a well-attended annual walking festival, and also specialist outdoor shops. This brand is very vulnerable to a crisis such as foot and mouth, since it needs countryside access.

Church Stretton is also known as 'Costa Geriatrica' but without the sea, as it is a retirement town with 55% of all inhabitants 'on pension'. It has a thriving cultural life, with over 50 community organisations. The compact Victorian town centre (it was formerly a spa town) has a very good range of shops, including a large antiques market.

Some people call the area 'Little Switzerland', as it is so attractive. There are numerous arts and walking festivals, the Longmynd Hike, and a food festival to support a thriving adventure tourism scene. There is even talk of developing a Malcolm Saville trail (named after the author of the *Lone Pine* stories about a group of children who had adventures in the area).

Craven Arms: 'Open for business — more than just a pub name'

Figure 4.25 New industrial estate on the site of the former market, Craven Arms

Craven Arms is the business centre of south Shropshire, as it is very accessible (rail and road junctions) and central to the whole district.

As part of the Market Towns Initiative a defunct auction yard was developed for mixed land use. Overall, Craven Arms offers several areas of affordable housing, as well as industrial estates with a range of small businesses, and a new Enterprise Centre. It has a range of basic services, including Tuffin's Superstore, a country supermarket developed on the site of the former market.

Craven Arms is also a tourism centre, home to the Shropshire Hills Discovery Centre, Stokesay Castle (a Medieval manor house), Acton Scott Farm Museum and Micky Miller's Play Barn. Although it is a very functional town and not especially pretty, it is a convenient place to stay as it is central to the whole area.

Cleobury Mortimer: 'Old fashioned and we are proud of it'

Figure 4.26 Cleobury Mortimer

The high street is one to remember — a long curving street of brick Georgian houses and shops interspersed with half-timbered buildings. Cleobury is no clone town, as it

has real bakers, butchers and ironmongers, all showing 'turn of the century charm'. The new Cleobury country rebrand markets the area as a quiet corner of rural England: a perfect place to unwind.

Cleobury is a tourist town famous for its church with a twisted spire, and a centre for walking in the Clee Hills. It has two hotels, a large activity centre and five pubs. While it is a pleasant, self-sufficient market town, many argue that it needs to rebrand, as they are very concerned about falling tourist trade and also the rapid growth in commuter housing on the brownfield site of a former engineering works.

Contemporary Case Studies

Questions

(a) Why did the south Shropshire towns need rebranding?

(b) Using evidence from the case study, explain which towns you think were the most and least successful rebrands? What fieldwork would you carry out to test your hunches? You should do an internet search for each town and look at their websites to gain extra information.

Guidance

(a) To provide extra employment from tourism and to ensure the services survive — to avoid becoming ghost towns.

(b) Successful rebrands build on the virtue of the old-fashioned market brand — yet some towns have more to offer in the first place. Diversity of brand is important too, to ensure year-round success.

Useful data might include primary fieldwork, health of town centre, footfalls, percentage of vacant shops, percentage of unemployment and tourism figures.

Examination advice

How to research rural environments effectively

Information about rural environments comes from a variety of sources: books, articles and websites (see pages ix–x). There is no one widely available magazine or periodical that specialises in rural geography, but many have useful articles about the countryside from time to time, such as the BBC's *Countryfile*. Radio programmes are very useful — especially programmes on BBC Radio 4 such as *Farming Today* and of course *The Archers*, which keep you up to date with key countryside issues. For rural areas in the developing world there are useful sources such as *Developments* magazine, published free, and various blogs from the frontline from charity workers.

There is a mass of information on the internet. Look for specialised podcasts, video clips on YouTube, and maps and aerial photographs from Multimap, Google Local and Google Earth. Always be aware of bias, especially if the material comes from an interest group, e.g. an environmental group such as CPRE or a pressure group such as the Countryside Alliance.

In developed rural environments primary research is both feasible and interesting. Suggested foci include:

■ studying change over time in rural environments — using your own detailed land-use surveys of farming and villages and then looking at historic maps to record and explain changes
■ assessing rural deprivation and inequality — Figure 5.1 shows how you can combine pre-visit secondary research fieldwork and post-fieldwork reviews

Figure 5.1
Rural deprivation in north Cornwall: sample field trip

Pre-visit

Google Earth can be used to establish the context of the investigation and explore the green fields, pretty villages and beautiful countryside of north Cornwall (Figure 5.2). The paradox of rural deprivation in the area can be explored using **www.cornwall.gov.uk**, which contains statistics of average

Figure 5.2
*Typical landscape of
north Cornwall*

wages for the county (among the UK's lowest). The Objective One website **www.objectiveone.com** has details of EU-funded programmes designed to improve Cornwall's outlook. Define the specific study area within Cornwall. The county has an excellent website — **www.cornwall.gov.uk** — that can be used with a GIS such as Google Earth to pinpoint villages for fieldwork survey. Ideally aim for systematic coverage of all settlements in a clearly defined study area. Background research can also be carried out using the Neighbourhood Statistics server of the ONS website at **www.statistics.gov.uk**. In particular, population profiles of areas can be investigated to examine the degree of ageing in the area, and the extent of young out-migration. Note that rural deprivation is rarely concentrated, unlike urban deprivation, which is frequently focused in ghettos and deprived wards.

Field trip

The self-sustaining spiral of rural disadvantage can be investigated by examining the degree of:

- resource deprivation
- opportunity deprivation
- mobility deprivation

1 Local job centres and connections, plus websites, can be visited to gauge the local jobs market and typical job types, contracts and wages. House price surveys (**http://news.bbc.co.uk/1/shared/spl/hi/in_depth/ukhouse_prices/html/houses.stm**) and housing quality surveys can be used: **www. upmystreet.com** is a useful source of additional local information. In Cornwall, a key issue is affordability: this could be investigated by a second homes survey, either directly or by questionnaire. Consider a shopping basket survey to gauge the cost of living in the area.

2 Services can be directly recorded using land-use surveys. Many services are 'hidden', so examine adverts in local papers and noticeboards in post offices and local stores. You can add to these surveys by using an online

Rural Development & the Countryside

Using case studies to write essays

There is a hierarchy of use, from examples (two or three factual sentences) to extended examples (paragraph length) to several short multiple case studies to a single detailed case study. So much depends on the exam context, but usually in a longer A2 essay-style answer several extended case studies or extended examples are required to develop and emphasise points in an argument.

(a) Deconstruct the title as shown below.

Critically assess the factors that are leading to change in remote upland rural areas.

You have to understand the **command word**, i.e. 'critically assess' — make a judgement, supported by evidence: in this instance extended examples would be useful. Extract **key words** — these could be topic key words (e.g. rural areas), place words (e.g. remote uplands) or issue key words (e.g. change and factors).

(b) Make a simple plan as shown below.

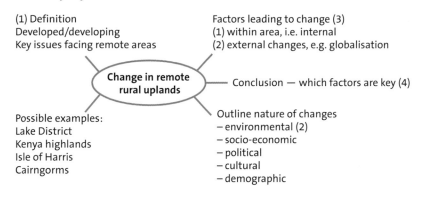

(1) Definition
Developed/developing
Key issues facing remote areas

Factors leading to change (3)
(1) within area, i.e. internal
(2) external changes, e.g. globalisation

Change in remote rural uplands

Conclusion — which factors are key (4)

Possible examples:
Lake District
Kenya highlands
Isle of Harris
Cairngorms

Outline nature of changes
– environmental (2)
– socio-economic
– political
– cultural
– demographic

(c) This could be further developed into a full structural sequence using a writing frame of an introduction (1), main body (2 and 3) and conclusion (4).

Avoid the case study by case study approach, as this can be very descriptive. It encourages long, rambling case studies not fully focused on the question, so if you think about the Lake District you can use the framework of nature of changes as shown below, always identifying the key factors responsible:

- environmental changes: deterioration of a landscape under threat from mass tourism
- socio-economic changes: struggle for survival of hill farming — disease, farm prices, McSharry reforms, diversification
- demographic changes: rural turnaround in accessible southern fringes, e.g. at Cartmel; some depopulation, e.g. Chapel Stile ghost village
- cultural changes: issue of declining services

- political changes: government energy policies impact outside national park on Energy Coast.

Always make sure that you write a conclusion which ties it all together.

(d) There are many different types of essay, so above all use the specification and exam board websites (which include examples of successful products) to really sort out what is required (style, timing, context etc.). Always have a good look at the mark scheme. For essays this will be a 'levels' mark scheme. The levels are distinguished by the quality of the essay structure, logicality and relevance of arguments, detail of exemplar support, effective use of geographical terminology and standards of written communication.

Index